She'd barely survived her last fight, and now her boss had saddled her with this...

The lock clicked as she opened the trunk and lifted the heavy Detroit steel. Carmine hated being right.

The package wasn't a package.

Brown eyes set in a wide, high cheek-boned, tan face blinked up at Carmine. The skinny bobcat girl from the arena, the Boss's flunky, was curled up in her trunk. Her pinstripe skirt was rumpled and her sleeveless silk blouse dusty from the ride.

"Shit!" Carmine slammed the trunk closed.

A muffled 'Hey!' came from the trunk followed by pounding fists.

Carmine leaned against the side of her car. She wanted to go home to her nice house in the East Hollywood Hills.

Her back itched from the healing stitches and her body ached. When she left the ring, she'd planned on a shot of tequila then bed.

Not this.

Not babysitting a skin walker until that crazy ass Naga could off a bunch of Yakuza. That wasn't her job. She was a prizefighter, not a gangster.

ROUND 1

Illegal pit fighter and werewolf Carmine Rojas gets an off-hours assignment from her boss—babysitting a skin walker who's gotten herself in trouble with the Yakuza. Carmine may kick ass in the ring but tangling with the Yakuza is well above her pay grade. So Carmine turns to her gangbanger cousin Rodrigo for help and firearms. Together they spend a terror-filled night battling Yakuza thugs, bickering over family, and blowing crap up.

ROUND 2

A martial-arts student of Carmine's finds an opportunity to make some much-needed money. What he doesn't know is how slim his chances are. Carmine must intervene or let him die. A tough choice, when intervening means asking her boss at the illegal fight club for help.

KUDOS for *Carmine Rojas: Dog Fight*

An explosive mix of gangsters, guns, monsters, magic and mayhem, with dark and gritty action that right-hooks you from page one. Wonderful! A howl-tastic mix of gangsters, guns, monsters, magic, and mayhem! – *Suzanne McLeod, author of the* Spellcrackers *urban fantasy series*

Ass-kicker by trade and nature, Carmine Rojas is a standout heroine in the urban fantasy field. Che Gilson brings a fresh take to the genre with an uncompromising voice and an action-packed plot that melds the fantastic with the all-too-real. A must read for fans of shape shifters, cage fighting, and good-old-fashioned, gripping storytelling. – *Naomi Clark, author of* Blood Hunt

I liked Carmine. She's very different from the heroines that we usually see in novels today. First of all she isn't beautiful, but instead, looks like a fighter whose nose has been broken numerous times. The book is a page turner and short enough to read in one sitting, which is a good thing, because once you pick it up, you won't be able put it down until you finish. – *Taylor Jones, Reviewer*

The characters are fun and the book is a page turner. But since it's short, I didn't even have to lose any sleep to get through it. If you want something that will make you laugh, make you groan, and get your heart rate up to a gallop, take a gander at *Carmine Rojas: Dog Fight*. – *Regan Murphy, Reviewer*

ACKNOWLEDGEMENTS

Thanks to everyone who read, critiqued, and commented on Carmine. Hopefully, you'll be up for help with the next one!

CARMINE ROJAS

DOG FIGHT

Che Gilson

A Black Opal Books Publication

GENRE: PARANORMAL THRILLER/ACTION-ADVENTURE

First Publication: JULY 2014

Published by Black Opal Books **http://www.blackopalbooks.com**

For Suzanne who's input, editing,
and help has been invaluable for years!

ROUND 1

CHaptER 1

The private locker room stank of years of un-
washed sweat and the blocked up toilet down
the hall. The aged fluorescent light overhead
flickered, making Carmine Rojas's eyes water.

The scent of blood drifted down the hall.

Twenty yards of green linoleum led to the fighting
pit.

Faint smacking sounds overlaid with the roar of the
crowd and the snarls of the fighters drifted through the
closed door.

In the arena Klaus "Ironfang" Weisman was beating bloody the latest fool to accept the open challenge.

A purse of $10,000 was a strong lure even though Klaus had killed three of his last ten challengers.

There was knock on the door. Carmine turned. A red-furred Kitsune came in, clawed toenails clicking loud enough that you could hear it down the hall.

His sharp fox muzzle grinned even though he slunk in, his body low in submission.

The fox bowed, pointed ears angled back and his tails tucked under the hem of his light cotton yukata robe.

The Kitsune was human enough in his shifted form to walk upright.

His low rank and meager magic meant he was subservient not only to Carmine but to the other foxes too. Fox magic was dependent on the number of tails they had.

With only three tails, the gofer sent to give her the message would never rise much farther. It was the silver nine-tails you had to watch out for. They had magic to spare and answered only to the Boss.

"You're up next, Rojas, time to get your fight on," he said.

A low rumble of anticipation vibrated in Carmine's chest. She got up from the wooden bench she'd been sitting on and towered over the smaller male.

As a human, Carmine wasn't much to look at, but her height drew stares—six feet, three inches tall and mistakenly called husky.

A very kind woman had once told her she looked Mayan and she should be proud. But hatchet noses, twice broken, didn't win beauty pageants.

"Get out," she told the fox, wanting him out of there before she changed.

He let out a staccato series of yips and bowed out. The door shut behind him.

She pulled the rubber band from her hair and let the black mane fall past her shoulders. Then she took off her robe.

Underneath was a racer-back tank with her fighting name, Lobo Negro in rhinestones across her chest and a pair of stretchy silk boxing shorts.

Reaching deep inside herself Carmine touched the wolf that was her other half.

Her heart raced as every muscle in her body cramped, doubling in size. The dull ache of her bones stretching and changing radiated soft pain throughout her body.

Already acute senses heightened. Fine black fur, dense and silky, sprouted and covered her body.

Transformation completed, Carmine snarled and punched the floor with a massive clawed hand. The sting in her knuckles helped her gather her senses. She pulled her thoughts together. Her body had changed but, unlike some shifters, her mind remained more or less intact.

Carmine dropped to all fours for a second and shook herself head to tail. Her half wolf form was something from a nightmare.

Mostly human, she could stand on two legs or run on all fours. Her hands became stubby clawed paws, thankfully leaving opposable thumbs intact.

All the better to grapple with opponents.

Her claws were sharp as razors and her grip was a vice.

A full-wolf form was out of the question though. The half wolf was the best that her strain of the curse allowed.

She scratched at her clothes to get her fur to sit right underneath the fabric and reared up, ears forward.

The crowd was screaming, their bloodlust at a fever pitch. Klaus must have won again.

Another knock at the door. One of the sleek, silver nine-tailed Kitsune pit masters entered. He bowed to her but was far less obsequious than his weaker cousin.

The fox couldn't hide a sly grin. "Your turn, Rojas. We've got a good one for you."

Her opponent was always a surprise. That was part of the challenge—one of the things that made her fights a main event. It was what the fans wanted to see.

Some wanted to watch her beat down anything the Boss threw at her. The rest wanted to see if at long last the Lobo Negro finally lost.

The Kitsune gestured and Carmine followed him out into the wide hall.

The metallic tang of blood in the air wet her mouth and made Carmine's nose twitch. She lifted her muzzle and inhaled deeply, letting the scent excite her.

Halfway down the hall she met Klaus, his iron-gray fur dyed red with blood. He was on all fours, favoring a wounded hind leg. A bloody flap of skin and muscle hung open.

Carmine dropped to all fours before she reached him. Her escort remained stiff backed but he stepped closer to the wall.

Klaus grunted a greeting at her as she passed. She grunted back and showed her throat to the older wolf as a sign of respect.

She let Klaus and his handlers, two mangy Kitsune who had themselves been fighters, and the fight club's patch-it man Dr. Herman pass before she continued on her way.

The hallway opened up into a T-junction where two other hallways met. The double doors that led to the fighting ring swung open and four beefy guys with a stretcher came out.

Klaus's latest victim. A featherweight coyote now a

pile of meat for the clean-up crew, ready for disposal in an oil drum to be tossed into the Pacific or buried in the desert.

Either way his remains would never be seen again. Still the coyote must have had some moves to tear open Klaus's leg like that.

The nine-tailed Kitsune grabbed one of the double doors as they swung shut.

Beyond was a dark tunnel thick with the odors of adrenaline and fear.

Carmine's heart raced, the prey smells igniting her blood.

Her ears flattened along her skull and a growl louder than an idling car shook the dust in the air.

There was one last door between her and the ring. The Kitsune held up a slender paw hand and Carmine waited. The silver fox stepped out to announce her.

The audience screamed as the Kitsune entered the arena.

Carmine ignored it. She had seen this act performed hundreds of times for her and all the other fighters.

The fight announcer came out, arms raised, and strutted around the ring, psyching up the audience.

Last minute bets were now being placed with the floor runners; sly red foxes, all of them quick with numbers.

The nine-tail's voice rang out over the loud speakers. "Ladies and gentlemen, shifters of all kinds, the moment you've all been waiting for! Tonight's main event! In this corner—"

Carmine burst through the door loping into the ring.

"We have ten-time undefeated champion, the Devil's black bitch herself, Lobo Negro, Carmine Rooooooojas!"

The Kitsune rolled his R's like a native.

Carmine snarled at the crowd, flashing three-inch, white canines.

She reared up to full height, seven and a half feet as a wolf, and let out a chilling hunting howl.

Applause broke over her. Fans chanted her name. She raked her claws through the air, soaking up the attention.

High above the floor of the ring, the stands were packed. A press of humans and shifters, all on their feet, stomped and cheered.

A few of the braver gamblers booed. In the midst of the waving sea of bodies, a small island of calm caught Carmine's eye.

A bunch of swanky skin walkers, their animal skins draped over pinstriped suits, frowned down at her. The tallest mage wore a bearskin.

The others were just wolves or coyotes, except for a sad-sack, skinny chick with a bobcat fur wrapped around her neck like a stole.

Rumor had it the pinstripe gang were "employees" of the Boss.

Though it was doubtful that they were employed for anything legal. Maybe that accounted for their lack of enthusiasm. The Boss might be displeased.

When the fox judged the crowd close to a frenzy, he gripped the mic suspended from the ceiling and pointed across the ring at the second door opposite from Carmine's entrance.

"And tonight's challenger, weighing in at a mere two-hundred-twenty pounds—" The Kitsune paused to let the crowd jeer. "—Ishiguro, Akikooooo, The White Wind!"

Ichi introduced the girl in Japanese fashion, last name first.

Carmine snapped her jaws as the challenger entered—a slim Okami, pale-brown fur shining sleekly over her muzzle and head as if groomed for a dog show not a bare-knuckle fight.

Her dazzling white kimono glowed against the filth of the underground fighting ring. She swept in, serene and confident, even at half Carmine's size. Her fawning Kitsune attendants, though employed by the fight club, carried the hem of her robe off the floor.

A few feet from Carmine, the Okami cast off her kimono. Underneath was a white karate uniform tailored to her wolf form.

Carmine looked up at the stands, past the rabble, higher, past the box seats where the money sat, all the way up to the dark-glassed owner's box.

The Japanese werewolves were the worst of surprises. If Carmine could have smiled, she would have. Okami were tricky and a novice fighter was sure be gutted in the first minute.

Carmine turned back to her opponent. The Okami's attendants were retreating.

The fox with the mic pulled a fan from the wide, indigo, kimono sleeve of his yukata. He held it poised as the Okami stepped up.

Carmine didn't even try to intimidate the Okami. That wasn't how you fought one. Besides, overconfidence was death in the ring. She would have to be quick and careful to come out of this alive.

"Bow and come out fighting," the fox said.

There was no need to explain the rules. There were no rules.

He held up the fan and snapped it open.

Carmine bowed to the self-styled White Wind. The Okami bent neatly at the waist.

"Aaaaand, FIGHT!"

The fox dropped the fan then somersaulted out of the ring. He landed on the edge of the stands ten feet above.

The first move was Carmine's. She'd learned from

fighting martial artists that it was the only way to get a fight started. All these kung-fu types would stand there until it snowed in hell.

Carmine lunged, starting with a right hook. Before her fist could connect, the Okami ghosted, disappearing into a thin white mist. Carmine knew the move. Her fist hit the ground and she balanced on it while kicking out with her back legs.

Her foot connected and she heard a surprised snarl. The weight against her foot was gone in a second.

The pungent ozone of the Okami's magic filled Carmine's mouth and nose. Scent would be useless in this battle and the crowd drowned out any sounds from Akiko herself.

Carmine dropped and swept her legs in a circle. There. Another contact. The Okami grunted as she fell, rolled, and ghosted out again.

Experience told Carmine she hadn't done any real damage.

A heavy weight dropped onto her from above, knocking her to the ground. An elbow drove into her kidney, making her howl. Then the weight was gone. Pain pulsated in her lower back.

Quickly, on all fours, she ran for the wall of the pit and backed against it.

Akiko was in the center ring, calm as a statue. Carmine's nose twitched. Was that a whiff of fear mixing with the burnt stink of magic? Or was it just wishful thinking?

Judging by the Okami's initial blitz attack, she hadn't expected to meet any resistance. She'd wanted to beat Carmine fast and hard for a quick win.

She was either new to the illegal fight circuit or arrogant. The Okami wouldn't make the same mistake twice.

The crowd's cheers shifted to angry boos and hisses, annoyed the fight had ground to a halt.

The Okami bowed again. Lower than she had before. Carmine's lips curled back, showing teeth. She would have respected Akiko if she'd fought fair.

A hail of plastic cups and wadded food wrappers pelted the Okami. Her gaze flicked up to the crowd. She ducked as someone threw an open beer can.

Carmine launched herself quick and low. She was over halfway to the Okami before Akiko noticed.

She ghosted out before Carmine reached her. Carmine didn't stop on the spot she'd occupied but shot past and began to circle.

Ghosting was a neat trick but the range and duration were limited. The magic was eating into the Okami's stamina, too.

The Okami re-materialized a few feet from where she had been standing, her back to Carmine.

Carmine leapt at the Okami, driving the slender

wolf to the ground, claws grappling for a hold. But she held nothing.

Carmine gagged on the ozone as it filled her mouth so thick she could taste it.

Akiko kicked Carmine in the face, a solid powerful blow. Carmine rolled with it, momentarily dizzy. Then she was up on all fours, trying to look everywhere at once.

Weight pressed her down. The Okami was on her back. An arm wrapped around Carmine's neck choking off the blood to her brain.

Akiko's hind legs kicked her. Clawed feet raked across Carmine's back, shredding the flesh.

Carmine stood, stretching to her full height, ignoring the pain and the threatening blackness. She toppled backward, using her body weight to slam the Okami into the ground.

Akiko squealed as the air was forced from her lungs. Carmine drove her elbow into Akiko's ribs until she felt something crack.

The chokehold broke just as Carmine's vision was tunneling out.

The raw agony, of fresh wounds hitting the packed dirt of the ring as she rolled away from the smaller wolf, cleared her vision.

Slower than she would have liked, Carmine got up, the thirsty dirt soaking up the red stain of her blood. The

Okami had retreated, her cool gone. The pale brown wolf snarled, one arm wrapped around her middle.

The question now was who could stand the most pain. Carmine's eyes swept over the Okami. The thin, graceful bitch was probably top of her class. She'd probably never lost a fight.

Until now.

Carmine barreled at the Okami. Akiko tried to ghost one more time, her outline growing hazy. Her magic was tapped out. She was solid when Carmine hit her.

Carmine pinned the Okami, gripped the lapel of her karate gi, and slammed her fist into her face. Again and again.

Akiko's muzzle and cheekbones broke under the onslaught. Carmine felt the bones shatter and tasted the Okami's blood as it sprayed into her mouth.

She wasn't sure what the Okami looked like human but judging from her smooth pelt and clean lines she was pretty.

Not anymore.

Another blow and her eye socket collapsed. Forget ugly, Carmine would leave her a corpse.

The air thickened around her as she pulled her fist back for the final blow. She was caught like an insect in molasses.

She managed to slowly turn her head.

The Kitsune announcer had jumped back into the ring. He had her locked in a spell.

Gold light lined the edges of his tails, which fanned out behind him.

The audience was enraged. Carmine heard their shouts and bellows as if from far away. Much more deadly ammunition was lobbed at him by the crowd than when the fight had paused earlier.

Glass bottles and unopened beer cans, thrown with sincere force, bounced off the ward the fox had erected around himself.

He stepped around the growing carpet of broken glass on tippy paws.

The crowd, denied a second death that night, was close to rioting. Enraged patrons in the stands assaulted the red fox bookies.

A folding chair hurtled through the air and clanged off the nine-tail's ward.

A sonic boom shook the arena. Carmine's ears popped.

Everything went still. The house lights flickered and the audience quieted. All eyes went to the dark-glassed owner's box.

"Carmine Rojas, Lobo Negro, is declared the winner. All bets will be honored. You may collect your winnings upstairs."

The voice booming out of the speakers was sexless.

Either a woman's deep voice or a man's high-pitched one. Impossible to tell.

Everyone obeyed as if it was the voice of God.

Even Carmine. She relaxed her body and the magic holding her loosened. She dropped the Okami and stood up.

The stretcher crew ran up as soon as Carmine was off her opponent. A doctor Carmine had never seen before checked the Okami's pulse.

He nodded and the stretcher-bearers gently lifted Akiko and put her on it.

Carmine watched them take her from the ring. If she wasn't meant to kill the Okami then the Okami had been meant to kill her.

Again, she looked to the owner's box. Maybe Carmine wasn't the draw she used to be.

A new champion initiated by blood was supposed to take over?

Honestly, Carmine would have just retired.

She left the ring on all fours, back stinging, leaving a snail trail of blood.

The house doctor met her at the tunnel exit.

"Come on, let's stitch up that back," he said around the cigarette clamped in his teeth.

CHAPTER 2

D r. Herman had a little exam room/operating theater in the fight complex. He could set bones, stitch up wounds, and do other minor repair work.

"Shift back and I'll close up those scratches. I ain't stitchin' through fur," Herman said.

He put out a tray of instruments but the stitching thread was already out. Compliments of Klaus no doubt.

Carmine stepped behind a screen and changed. Like most shifters, she didn't want anyone seeing the transition.

She wasn't sure why.

Even more than nudity, it seemed private, some-how. The shift didn't normally hurt but the wounds stung like lemon juice had been poured down her back.

Human again, Carmine came out.

"Face down." Dr. Herman pointed to the exam ta-ble. "How's the kidney?"

"I'll live."

She lay on her stomach while the Doc cut off the remains of her top.

He stitched her up without anesthetic. The massive doses of specialized drugs it took to put a werewolf un-der were cost prohibitive.

Even having a doctor meant this fight operation was already the Ferrari of illegal fight clubs.

Carmine had spent years fighting in places that were little more than abandoned warehouses, temporari-ly re-purposed. She'd made it to the top, all right.

"Get someone to take these out in a day or two and give me a call if you get a fever."

Luckily, werewolves healed fast. She counted one hundred seventy eight stitches. The Okami's claws had gone to the bone.

"Sit up," Herman ordered. He wound gauze band-ages around her mid-section and up over her breasts to cover her entire back. There was a knock at the door.

"Yeah?" Herman said, loud enough to be heard by a human on the other side.

The exam room door opened. Another nine-tails. Carmine knew them all by scent but they never used names only numbers, which were sewn onto the backs of their yukata. The numbers corresponded with their closeness to the mysterious Boss.

Carmine's brown-black eyes narrowed when they confirmed what her nose had told her.

The Kitsune was Ichi, number one, the closest to the Boss. He always smelled of musk, spicy smoke, and reptiles.

Needle sharp teeth glinted as Ichi grinned. "You've been requested."

Her stomach knotted tight. *No one* saw the Boss—at least no one at Carmine's level.

She'd never dealt with anyone other than the managers and arena staff. Not a pattern she wanted to break.

Not after an attempt on her life.

If she didn't say yes, Ichi would spell her and drag her upstairs.

"Let me get some clothes on. Meet me outside my locker room."

Ichi nodded and left. There was no way for Carmine to get away and she knew it.

"Off to see the wizard?" Dr. Herman grunted.

"Guess so."

"I'd say be careful if it'd help."

"You ever meet the Boss?"

"No. It's so if we all get caught, we don't know anything."

As she thought. Which meant meeting the Boss might assure her death. She didn't even get a last meal.

Carmine eased herself off the exam table. The thought that she should have run the instant she left the ring crossed her mind.

Not that it would have helped.

At least, she could have taken out a few of those smug Kitsune before going down. But then her corpse would be sharing that oil drum with the coyote.

Two-for-one burial.

She went back to the locker room and pulled out the clothes she'd arrived in. Black jeans and a loose T-shirt. Easy on the wounds.

The only standout item she wore was a pair of snakeskin cowboy boots.

Carmine pulled her hair into a ponytail and threw the boxing shorts into her sports bag. Doc Herman had tossed the remains of her fight top in the trash.

She poked her head out the door, half hoping the fox wouldn't be there.

"Ready?" Ichi asked.

Carmine nodded.

He led her down the hall toward the arena but turned left where it branched.

They went upstairs to the lobby where patrons

waited until the doors to the ring opened for the show—
a wide space with a diamond marquise floor.

There was another corridor behind a locked door
that read *JANITOR*.

Ichi led her up a couple flights of stairs to a door
with a matched pair of muscle guarding it.

Carmine hesitated and sniffed the air. The knot in
her stomach became a cramp.

Tiger sorcerers. Their bronze skin exuded the scent
of magic, making them smell like the minutes before a
thunderstorm.

Underneath was the stink of big cat, pheromones,
and rotting meat.

They could change into tigers as fast as the Okami
could ghost—faster than Carmine could change.

The left hand tiger had five inches on Carmine and
was twice as wide. Muscles strained the seams of his
black suit. He looked down at Carmine and Ichi.

The oily feel of magic touched her skin. She felt the
magic roam over her body, looking for weapons, and
she swallowed a growl.

The magic dissolved and the tiger nodded to his
buddy. He opened the door.

Warm air brushed against Carmine. The sandalwood reek of incense and the peculiar swamp smell of
reptile overwhelmed her nose.

Ichi led the way to a dark chamber that was an extravagant mix of Kasbah and Indian bazaar. Bright magenta, blue, purple, and green sari silks draped like a tent roof across the ceiling.

Star-shaped lanterns of colored glass cast patches of garish light on the Turkish rugs that padded the floor. The only places to sit were enormous floor pillows strewn about the room.

A group of stiff-backed Japanese men, including the doctor from the ring, knelt on the pillows. *They must be with the Okami.* Carmine inhaled.

There—the gray-haired man who sat in the center of the others. He was Okami, too.

She saw his nostrils flare just a fraction. His head didn't move but she knew he'd sniffed her out.

The million-dollar question was did he know she was the wolf from the ring?

He could smell the blood on her, to be sure, but for all he knew, it could just be her period. But the coincidence was too much. Which didn't explain why the old man hadn't tried to snap her neck by now.

He had Yakuza stamped across his forehead. Of course, she hadn't killed Akiko so maybe the same courtesy was being extended to her.

Across the room, two more tigers stood in front of a door obscured by gaudy silk. Ichi gestured at them and one of the tigers opened the door.

CHaptER 3

Hot air hit Carmine like a wall and the pungent salmonella scent of reptile increased a thousand fold. All the incense in the world couldn't have covered that smell.

The room was lit with red bulbs that threw more heat than light. Her eyes took a second to adjust to the bloody twilight.

Carmine froze. She was in the owner's box. The Boss was silhouetted against a floor to ceiling window. Below she could see the cleanup crew sweeping broken glass from the ring.

The figure turned and everything in the room

moved. What Carmine had taken to be more floor pillows were the coils of a snake.

She took a step back and heard the door close behind her. The sound sent a spike of ice through her. Ichi had left her alone.

Alone with a Naga.

But how? The only river in L.A. was that paved trickle running through downtown.

The Naga slithered into the light, and all around the room, the coils of snake tail shifted with a dry raspy sound.

"A pleasure to finally meet you, Miss Rojas," said a smoky voice.

The snake was a woman. Dark-brown skin picked up the ruby light of the heat lamps. Long black hair, piled in fancy braids, wrapped around her head.

Her nose was pierced with a gold hoop, and a chain went from nose to ear. She wore a sari over a skimpy bikini top and, most importantly, she was snake from the waist down.

Gleaming, flat belly scales and an acre of ribs and muscle propelled her forward. Eyes as black as Carmine's looked her up and down.

Carmine regretted the snakeskin boots. "You must be the Boss," she said.

Her body was tight, straining to run, but she forced herself to stay still.

She held out her hand. "Sejal Johar."

Carmine hesitated. She looked at the long curving nails painted violet and sparkling with tiny gems.

"You may call me Sejal," the Naga said.

Carmine couldn't stare at the Naga's hand forever. She shoved her fear aside and shook it. The skin was warm and the grip surprisingly strong.

"You must be wondering why I asked you up here," Sejal said as she released Carmine's hand.

Carmine decided to cut through the chitchat. "Is it to kill me?"

The Naga's eyes flashed, lighting from within. For a second, Carmine could see the slit pupils silhouetted against the glow.

Sejal laughed. A hissing throaty sound. Her coils rasped. She slid closer to Carmine and tasted the air with a forked tongue.

"I didn't think the great Lobo Negro would be afraid," Sejal smiled. "But you're still brave, my champion. I chose well."

Nothing the Naga had said so far was even a little reassuring.

"Can you just tell me what's going on?"

Sejal's good humor didn't fade. Her smile stretched wider.

"I like you, Carmine. I've always liked you. The three years you've been here I've never missed a fight.

You've never backed down from anything I've thrown at you."

"The Okami was meant to kill me," Carmine growled.

"Ssss. Ssss." Sejal held up a hand and Carmine snapped her mouth shut. "A wager. Not a friendly one," she said. "Someone I protect has run afoul of the Yakuza in the next room. We each put a champion in the ring. Unfortunately for us all, he put in his daughter."

Carmine's fists clenched. She'd dealt with gangs and mobsters all her life. Posturing and arrogance was all they cared about. They'd put their mothers in the ground if they thought it'd up their street cred.

Now she was stuck on some kind of clean-up duty, or worse. Too bad Sejal didn't seem to want to spit out a straight answer.

Carmine's nails dug a little deeper into her palms. She was just a prizefighter, for entertainment only. Until now.

"Ishiguro lost and the win goes to me but that won't stop him," Sejal said. "He's been in America too long and forgotten his honor. He will strike at you and at me. There is a package in the trunk of your car. Take it somewhere safe. Open it only away from prying eyes. I just need enough time to contact Ishiguro's bosses in Osaka. If they have honor left, they'll cut him off and I can deal with him."

Carmine thought of the four tiger sorcerers at the doors and wondered how many more Sejal had stashed away.

So Sejal would take care of the Yakuza but, still, that left Carmine with the mystery package. Whatever it was it had to be illegal.

Or dangerous.

She tried to imagine what it could be—guns, drugs, a body? Clenching her teeth, she quit while she was ahead.

She nodded at the door she'd come through. "Do they know who I am?"

"I haven't told them but they can put two and two together. The tigers will keep them from moving, for now."

"They'll come with silver. I can't do anything about that."

Despite appearances, Carmine was descended from European wolves. The Conquistadors brought the were-curse to the Americas and passed it onto their native mistresses and children.

Sejal's grin widened enough to show fang. "I can help with that."

She moved faster than Carmine could see. The snake tail coiled around Carmine, squeezing her arms to her body. She didn't even have time to panic before Sejal pressed her lips to Carmine's.

The Naga's skin was hot against Carmine's face, the gold chain of the nose ring a chilling slash against her cheek. Sejal's forked tongue pushed into Carmine's mouth, parting her teeth. Something warm and prickly hit Carmine's tongue. A sticky ball of energy that squirmed in her mouth, leaving the bitter taste of metal and sandalwood. Carmine gagged, trying to fight it.

Sejal's hand stroked her throat. "Just swallow," she murmured in Carmine's ear.

Carmine did. The ball of magic nettled down her throat and expanded in her stomach. Heat suffused her body and cold sweat broke over her skin.

The coils holding Carmine fell away and she doubled over, wheezing.

"That charm will make you immune to silver for a couple days. With luck, everything will be settled before then."

"There's no choice, is there?" Carmine panted. "I have to do this."

The effects of the charm were dissipating and she straightened up.

"Afraid so." Sejal managed to sound a little sorry. She slithered over to the wall by the windows and pulled aside the draped silk. "This door will take you to the parking garage. I wouldn't go home, if I were you."

"This is insane," Carmine snarled. "You're insane. I can quit."

The Naga smiled, her teeth white against her skin. "You can quit tomorrow—if you're still alive."

Carmine's lip curled. She was on the verge of changing but pulled back. There was no time to wipe the smirk off Sejal's face and it was unlikely she even could. The choice had been made for her.

Working an illegal fight club didn't exactly give her a lot of options. But real sports, professional sports with sponsors, didn't allow shifters.

So it was Sejal or nothing. And now, it seemed, she was stuck with a few extra-curricular activities.

Carmine opened the door and followed the concrete stairs. The stairwell dead-ended four flights up at a steel door. She put her ear to the door in case she could hear anything beyond. Nothing.

She opened the door.

The underground parking garage was the secret entrance to the fight club. Carmine came out on level five in an area she'd never parked in before.

She looked at the door as she came out of it. *Maintenance* was stenciled across it in white spray paint. Clever.

Green fluorescent bulbs cast watery shadows around the garage. There were a few parked cars that could easily hide an ambush but Carmine heard nothing.

She walked quickly up the ramp, her ears and nose on alert.

She picked up the faint smell of the crowds that had been there earlier and the piercing stink of motor oil and exhaust.

Carmine made it to her car, an enormous land yacht of a Ford Galaxie.

She had her car keys in her hand. The temptation to open the trunk stopped her in her tracks.

What was it? Drugs? A body?

She sniffed the air but all she got was the scent of the garage. As a wolf, she could have told what was in there, but not now.

Besides, she had to get out of there. The car was a beacon, one of the few ostentations she'd let herself have.

The glitter paint job was dark blue with orange flames streaking up the side. And on the hood, custom painted for her, was a snarling black wolf head.

She only drove it to fights and sometimes took it cruising to show off. Her regular car was in the rented space the Galaxie normally occupied in a parking garage a few miles away.

Carmine decided to go get her normal car first then figure out what to do. Maybe she could just leave the Galaxie and the "package" in the garage.

She got in and started the car. The engine rumbled and Carmine drove as fast as possible out of the parking garage.

Chapter 4

When she hit the streets of downtown L.A., all bets were off. Carmine wasn't a cop or a criminal.

She didn't know how to tell if anyone was following her. She kept checking the rearview mirror, but the streets were as empty as they ever got in Los Angeles.

It was closing in on 2 a.m. and traffic was light. Downtown didn't have much to offer this late. The tacky rundown stores with names all in Spanish were gated and dark.

The real action would be in Hollywood, in the clubs and bars swarming with limos and celebutantes.

Carmine took surface streets all the way to the circular towers of the Bonaventure Hotel where she rented her long-term parking spot.

The freeway seemed like it would be an easy route to follow if the Yakuza muscle were right behind her.

Of course, she could be wrong.

Her fists clutched the welded, chrome-covered chain of the steering wheel until her knuckles turned Caucasian.

The financial district was even quieter than downtown and the streets were nearly deserted. The 9-to-5 regulars had all gone home long ago.

She was halfway to the Bonaventure when she hit a rougher than usual pothole in the road.

She felt a significant weight in the trunk shift and roll.

Then her ears picked up a muffled sound. Carmine's foot eased off the gas.

Was she imagining things, or had she heard a voice from the trunk?

Carmine pulled over in front of a locked-down bank with a metal fence pulled across the front of it. She cut the engine and listened hard.

There.

A grunt and another thump. Son of a bitch, something *was* back there.

Something alive and moving.

Carmine went cold. Kidnapping was a federal offense. Forget regular prison. She'd be in a fancy silver-plated eight-by-six in a federal super max.

What the hell, had Sejal gotten her in to?

She hesitated a second longer, hands glued to the steering wheel. Which was worse? Knowing? Or not knowing? A shit choice to be sure.

Unfortunately, ignorance wasn't much of a defense if she was caught by the cops or the Yakuza. Carmine took a deep breath and pulled her hands off the wheel. She took the keys from the ignition and climbed out of the car.

She was tempted to just pop the trunk from the cabin and let whatever was in there make a run for it. But Sejal would probably have something to say about that.

The lock clicked as she opened the trunk and lifted the heavy Detroit steel. Carmine hated being right.

The package wasn't a package.

Brown eyes set in a wide, high cheek-boned, tan face blinked up at Carmine.

The skinny bobcat girl from the arena, the Boss's flunky, was curled up in her trunk. Her pinstripe skirt was rumpled and her sleeveless silk blouse dusty from the ride.

"Shit!" Carmine slammed the trunk closed.

A muffled 'Hey!' came from the trunk followed by pounding fists.

Carmine leaned against the side of her car. She wanted to go home to her nice house in the East Hollywood Hills.

Her back itched from the healing stitches and her body ached. When she left the ring, she'd planned on a shot of tequila then bed.

Not this.

Not babysitting a skin walker until that crazy ass Naga could off a bunch of Yakuza. That wasn't her job. She was a prizefighter, not a gangster.

The thumps and pounding from the trunk continued. "Hey! Please let me out! Sejal said you'd protect me. Please! You can't do this!"

Carmine opened the trunk. The bobcat girl's fist froze as Carmine snarled at her. "Don't scratch my car."

The girl shrank back. Carmine reached into the trunk and grabbed the waistline of her skirt.

She hauled the bobcat out like luggage and dropped her to the concrete. She sprawled on the broken sidewalk, staring up at Carmine in terror. Then she sprang to her feet, landing neatly on her spiked hooker heels.

Even on five-inch heels the girl barely came up to Carmine's chest.

The bobcat backed up a step. "Are you going to put me back in the trunk?" she asked.

"Maybe," Carmine said.

"Sejal told you to help me, right?"

"She wasn't real specific."

"She was, you're lying," the bobcat said.

Her voice was firm but Carmine could see the pale under her tanned skin and smell her fear.

"What's your name?" Carmine asked.

"Ooljee Natseway."

"You're a long way from the Rez." The Navajo Reservation was one state over from Cali, occupying a good chunk of Arizona and New Mexico.

"Screw you! We don't all live on a reservation."

"What did you do to the Yakuza?"

"You really wanna know?"

Carmine sighed. "Not really."

"Well, I only took it because it was shiny anyway," Ooljee blurted. "How was I supposed to know it was a freakin' museum piece? I mean it's a bronze mirror. Not silver or something."

"Stealing from a Yakuza boss?" Carmine growled and pinched the bridge of her nose. She didn't even know where to start.

What was worse? Stealing a museum-grade bronze mirror in the first place, or stealing it just because it was "shiny"? Was she a bobcat or a magpie?

They were silent a minute while Carmine tried to get a handle on her impulse to strangle the girl.

Ooljee eyed her askance, sizing her up. The bobcat was tense. Ready to bolt, hooker heels or not.

Unless she had a better trick than turning into a bobcat up her sleeve, she wasn't going anywhere.

"What do we do now?" she asked.

She still kept her distance but she relaxed a little. She'd apparently either decided that it was safer to stay with Carmine or realized she couldn't get away.

Carmine thought about that. She didn't know much about Yakuza beyond that they liked tattoos and were well organized.

"How good are they at tracking? Do they have your scent?"

Ooljee pouted. If she was going for disarming, she was way off. Maybe that worked on guys, but Carmine wasn't buying it.

Carmine took a step closer. "What?"

The girl squirmed and didn't answer. Her gaze dropped to the street.

Carmine's hand darted out. She grabbed Ooljee's arm, digging her fingers into the bobcat's flesh and squeezing until she felt bone.

If the girl didn't start talking faster, they were both going to be dead. Horribly dead, the way only mobsters could manage.

Ooljee hissed and cried out in pain. Her free hand reached up to her neck to touch the bobcat pelt wrapped around her shoulders but Carmine caught her wrist.

"I want an answer," she said, her voice low.

"My blood." Ooljee whimpered in pain. "They have my blood."

Carmine fought down the urge to punch Ooljee in the face. She should be mad at Sejal, who had put her in the situation.

With the girl's blood, they could track her anywhere. There were dozens of spells and scrying techniques they could use.

"We have to get out of here!"

Carmine was close to shouting. Panic and rage battled inside her. She dragged Ooljee to the Ford and threw her in the passenger side.

"Stay." Carmine shook a finger at her and slammed the door. "*¡Puto hija de puta!*" she cursed as she hurried around to the driver's side.

Carmine got in and revved the engine. The Ford shot forward and she peeled out, tires squealing in protest.

The heavy old Ford was never meant for speed. Ooljee buckled her seat belt and wisely said nothing.

The freeway seemed like the best bet now. She needed to move fast. Was Sejal still stalling Ishiguro? Maybe he was waiting for Number One Daughter to wake up.

As Carmine reached the 101 Freeway entrance, she realized she was still swearing in Spanish.

She switched to English. "Goddamn son of a bitch!

The Okami has your blood! Why wasn't that the first thing out of your mouth?"

Ooljee scrunched against the passenger door, shrinking from the force of Carmine's rage. "I'm sorry. I know I should have."

Carmine considered grabbing the bobcat and inflicting a little more damage.

Dark reddish bruises were already blooming on her upper arm and wrist. But they hit the freeway and Carmine had to concentrate on driving.

She gunned the Ford, pushing it up to seventy then eighty. She could practically see the gas gauge going down. The Galaxie was a monster gas hog.

Carmine didn't believe in God but she looked at the rosary hanging from the rearview mirror and prayed to reach her destination.

"Where are we going?" Ooljee asked.

"My *tia* Graciela's house. They live in El Sereno."

"They?"

"My cousin Rodrigo is a gang banger. A real one. A lieutenant. He'll help us."

"Is he a werewolf?"

"Yes."

Shifter gangs were the scourge of Los Angeles. Unstoppable. Feral. The poor neighborhoods they savaged couldn't afford the silver-plated bullets for werewolves like the cops could.

They had to make do with what silver they could get to coat or stud blunt weapons, mace made with wolfs bane, and protective charms from the local bruja.

Not that the police didn't employ their own shifters and sorcerers. But there were places in L.A. that the police just didn't go. El Sereno was one.

Despite the gentrification of a number of East L.A. neighborhoods, El Sereno remained untamed, split into gang territories, held by men like her cousin.

Carmine saw the exit and got off the freeway. Ooljee kept looking behind them.

"Can you tell if we're being followed?" Carmine asked.

"Sort of. I don't think we are. Not yet. You messed up that bitch pretty bad. Daddy will wait till she's conscious to come after us. I think."

Carmine glanced at Ooljee. "Do you know how to kill an Okami?"

She nodded. "Cutting off the head is the easiest. That's why they all run around with samurai swords."

That sounded about right. There was probably an herbal repellent or two but Carmine didn't know what they were.

"How many Okami does Ishiguro have?"

"There's just the old man and his daughter," Ooljee said. "But he has plenty of thugs."

Humans were easier to deal with than shifters.

"Sorcerers?"

"Shinto priest guy, scries with fire."

"You better get a little quicker with the answers or I'll plant you in the ground myself," Carmine said.

"Sejal—"

Carmine punched the dashboard. "Sejal can go fuck herself!"

Ooljee cringed and Carmine wasn't sorry one bit. The girl stroked her bobcat pelt for comfort and Carmine turned back to the road and realized she didn't quite know where she was.

Rundown houses blurred past, security doors locked, windows blockaded with bars. The fences were chain-link and the lawns brown in the light of the street lamps.

Rottweilers and pit bulls on heavy chains barked as the car drove past.

Carmine dredged the address up from memory and realized she was about eight blocks off, in the wrong direction.

Two right turns later and she was headed the right way.

"Anything behind us?" Carmine asked.

Ooljee turned around in her seat. Her eyes went catty for a second, gold and slit-pupiled. "Nothing," she said.

"Keep watching."

Carmine counted off the darkened blocks as she drove. She needed to explain something to Ooljee before they reach her cousin's house.

"Ooljee," Carmine said.

Her foot eased on the accelerator and the Galaxie slowed to a crawl.

"What?"

"My family doesn't know what I do for living."

A canary-eating grin spread across Ooljee's face. "Really?"

That was exactly the reaction Carmine had been dreading. "I can wipe that smirk off your face anytime."

Ooljee's grin disappeared, but Carmine could see her lips twitching.

"They think I work for a consulting firm that helps companies target marketing to Hispanic buyers."

The bobcat blinked. "That's specific."

"I came up with it myself. In my spare time, I coach mixed martial arts and boxing at a gym. Whatever I tell my aunt and my cousin about you has to fit into that."

The grin tugged at the corner of Ooljee's mouth. "Lobo Negro takes the smart money. Who'd have thought it?"

Carmine reached across the seat and slapped Ooljee's arm. The blow was light but still knocked the girl into the vinyl-paneled door. Ooljee rubbed her arm.

"Ow! I just meant no one ever takes the smart money, is all."

There were two ways to get paid your winnings at the fight club.

Cash on the spot, which all but Carmine and a couple other fighters took, or the smart money.

Carmine was on the books of a shell corporation that paid her to be a consultant.

She declared the money on her taxes, had a bank account, and paid off her house, all above board.

The ones who took the upfront money weren't always so lucky.

They ended up with IRS troubles or got robbed because they couldn't deposit the cash in a bank.

Some, like Klaus, spent the money as fast as they got it.

"I'm surprised more of the fighters don't do it like you do," Ooljee said.

"It cuts into the profits to have it laundered." Carmine's winnings took a twenty to thirty percent hit. "Not that it's any of your business. So what cover story do I tell my aunt about you?"

"Well I'm not going to be from your gym." Ooljee's forehead wrinkled with what Carmine hoped was thought. She wiggled her narrow hips. "I'm a lover not a fighter."

"Gym it is," Carmine frowned.

Ooljee looked incredulous. "What?"

"Some fighters' girlfriends get involved with the mob. I've seen it before. Gambling debts or something."

Head cocked, Ooljee considered. "Good enough," she said at last.

Carmine pulled the Ford over to the curb. Beyond the sagging chain-link fence was an ocher-colored house. Paint peeled off the craftsman-style beams.

A bathtub shrine to the Virgin Mary rose out of brown grass—the old Victorian soaker tub sawed in half and planted in concrete.

Rust showed through the peeling enamel and the plaster Virgin under its domed shelter was chipped and faded. Solar garden lights lit it from within.

"We're here," she said.

She cut the engine but didn't get out of the car. She hardly spoke to her aunt or cousin.

They were the poor relatives she had worked hard to distance herself from.

A life she once shared.

A reminder she didn't appreciate.

Ooljee bounced out of the car. She smoothed her blouse and arranged the thigh high slit in her skirt.

"How do I look?"

She bent over and looked in the passenger side window under the delusion that Carmine cared.

Without replying, Carmine got out and locked the

door. Lifting her head, she scented the air, ears alert for danger.

The faint scent of stale cooking met her nose. Beans and grease, the garbage cans behind the detached garage, and the animal musk of other shifters.

"Come on," she said, her voice a whisper above inaudible.

She opened the gate, which squeaked on rusted hinges.

Ooljee was right on her heels, so close she collided with Carmine when she stopped at the front door.

For all Ooljee's apparent flippantness, Carmine could smell the fear coming off the bobcat.

CHAPTER 5

Carmine rang the doorbell. The front door had a brass knocker as well but it was safe from use behind a steel security screen.

She was about to ring the bell again when the door whipped open.

A gun barrel poked between the security door bars. Ooljee squealed and ducked behind Carmine.

Raising her arms slowly Carmine said, "Hi, Rodrigo."

"What the fuck? Carmine?"

"Carmine?" came a higher pitched echo from inside the darkened house.

A light switched on.

"I told you to keep it off, Mama," Rodrigo yelled over his shoulder.

"You just said it's Carmine."

"Um," Carmine said.

The gun was still aimed at her face. She didn't know what additions his ammo had but she didn't want to find out, silver proofed by Sejal's charm or not.

He turned back to Carmine, brown eyes sweeping over her. He wore nothing but boxer shorts and socks, so he must've just gotten out of bed.

A gold crucifix hung against his chest, right next to the puckered scars of healed bullet wounds.

Rodrigo kept the gun level with her face. "What do you want?"

"Put that away," ordered Graciela.

She came up behind Rodrigo and pushed his arm down.

Carmine inhaled sharply waiting for the gun to go off, muscles tensed in case she had to throw herself out of the way.

Not that there was anywhere to go. She'd be a sitting duck on that brown square of lawn

Rodrigo snapped the gun back up. "Mama!"

Graciela looked older than Carmine remembered. The thick braid that hung over her shoulder used to be pure black. Now silver threaded through it. The bags under her weary eyes were gray stains against the copper of her skin.

"She's your cousin," Graciela said firmly.

She shoved past Rodrigo, bumping him aside with an ample hip. Rodrigo snarled with disgust and put his hands up in surrender.

With the gun now aimed at the ceiling, Carmine exhaled in relief. Graciela unlocked the security door as Rodrigo retreated.

"Come in, come in," she said. She pulled Carmine into a big unwanted hug. "*Cariño*, it's been forever."

Caught off guard, Carmine stiffened. If Graciela noticed, she didn't let go.

Her aunt only come up to Carmine's chest but her arms were like steel bands around her waist.

After a long second of hesitation, she relaxed and returned the hug.

"She's too good for us now."

Rodrigo crossed the scuffed tile floor in two long strides and flopped down on a threadbare couch. He kept the 9mm in hand.

Graciela made a dismissive grunt and let Carmine go. "Now, who's your friend?"

"Skin-walker, Mama. You can smell her from here."

"I asked who not what," Graciela said.

Carmine stepped aside so Ooljee could come in.

The bobcat entered delicately, sniffing. Faint disdain came off her moves.

It may have been her inner bobcat emerging but, judging by the cut of her clothes, she probably wasn't used to slumming it.

Not that Carmine could throw stones. Rodrigo's assessment that she was too good for them now was fair, if cutting.

She wouldn't be there if she didn't need guns and muscle.

"Evening," Ooljee said. She picked her way around the room like a house cat, eyeing whatever caught her attention. "Pleased to meet you. I'm Ooljee Natseway."

She moved by instinct, leaning over to sniff the smells coming from a recliner covered in lace doilies. Maybe Carmine was alone in her disdain.

"Nice to meet you, Ooljee, I'm—"

"Sorry, Graciela," Carmine cut her off. She turned to Rodrigo. "I need your help."

"I knew you weren't here 'cause you miss us."

"Ooljee is in trouble with the Yakuza."

Ooljee came over to Carmine and stood next to her, one leg slightly forward to show off the slit in her skirt.

Rodrigo's suspicious look flicked from Carmine's face to Ooljee's bare leg.

"It's all because of my cheating boxer boyfriend," Ooljee said.

She leaned forward, seeming to forget her blouse showed no cleavage. Because she didn't have any.

"Soon to be ex-boyfriend."

The stupid grin spreading on Rodrigo's face told Carmine he was hooked.

"*Pobre bebé*," he said. "You need money? Drugs? What?"

"Guns and protection," Carmine said.

The stupid grin dissolved. "Spill it."

"Carmine was just defending me. It's not her fault."

Ooljee put herself in front of Carmine. A nice gesture that meant nothing. It would take a linebacker to shield her.

"The Boss's daughter showed up at the gym for payback and Carmine saved me, but she beat Ishiguro real bad. They're coming after us."

"Ishiguro? Aren't they Okami?" Rodrigo jumped off the couch. He gestured at Carmine with the 9mm. "You beat up a Yakuza wolf then drag your shit to my door? My mom's here, my little sister—"

"Angela's at a friend's house," Graciela cut in.

"That don't matter!" he shouted.

"Please," Ooljee begged, her hands in the air. "We'll pay you! My skin-walker clan has money."

Rodrigo's gaze traveled up and down Ooljee's body, lingering on the tan stretch of leg showing through her skirt, then returned to her face.

"You'll pay, all right." He pointed the gun at Carmine. "I want your car, that sweet ass Ford you got parked outside."

Carmine considered trying to disarm Rodrigo and pounding his head into the floor until it burst like a watermelon.

But the gun could go off and hit Graciela or her.

"Fine."

Her voice was flat with rage, all her effort going into not changing.

"And you." Rodrigo lowered the gun and grinned at Ooljee. "I wanna date. Don't worry. A nice one. I'm a gentleman."

Carmine snorted.

The gun leveled with her face again.

"Something to say, Carmine?"

"No."

"Didn't think so." He turned back to Ooljee. "So how about it, kitty cat?"

She smiled. "Sure."

Rodrigo nodded. "All right."

He sidled a little closer and Ooljee giggled.

Carmine had to put the brakes on this before she vomited.

"You can't date her if she's dead."

"Oh, right." Rodrigo snapped back to attention. "Gimme your car keys."

Slower than intended, Carmine dug into her pocket. She loved that Galaxie. The custom paint job—she didn't want to think about how much she'd spent on it.

"Wait here while I get some clothes on." He gave Ooljee a parting wink. "See if they want anything, Mama."

"Would you like anything? A soda?" Graciela asked when her son was gone.

"You don't have to wait on us, Graciela."

"I'd like some water," Ooljee said.

"Sure." Graciela headed for the kitchen to the right of the living room.

"Your cousin's cute," Ooljee said.

Carmine rolled her eyes. "You two deserve each other, I'm sure."

Graciela came back with a glass of water for Ooljee.

"Thanks, Mrs…"

"Graciela is fine," she said.

"You shouldn't let Rodrigo talk to you like that."

Graciela waved away Carmine's concern and sat down on the doily-covered chair.

"I'm sorry. Rodrigo is right," Carmen said. "I brought this to your door."

Graciela looked at Carmine, a sad look in her hound-dog eyes. "You're always welcome, *cariño*. I just wish you knew that."

There was nothing that Carmine could or wanted to say.

She loved her aunt but not her life.

Not her family.

Her two oldest boys Javier and Alejandro were in different prisons, her third kid, Lucia, was married to a thug and lived in Watts.

Rodrigo would be the next guest of Corcoran State Prison, the way he was going.

The thought was hypocritical, since he was the first one Carmine came to for help.

Of course, she would be in prison too if anyone blew the whistle on the fight club. Not to mention the stack of bodies she'd left behind over the years.

Carmine grimaced as she watched Ooljee down the glass of water. If it wasn't for her, Carmine would be home, not sitting in uncomfortable silence in Graciela's living room.

"So you're Carmine's aunt," Ooljee said. "What's that like?"

"Don't—shut up, Ooljee," Carmine said.

Graciela smiled. "She was a very…determined little girl."

Ooljee giggled. "That's code for stubborn."

"As a burro," Graciela said.

"Okay, enough. Ooljee, thank *Tia* Graciela for the water. We're waiting by the car."

Ooljee put the water glass down on a battered end table. "Thank you, *Tia* Graciela."

Carmine was relieved to see Rodrigo come back. He'd pulled on a white, wife-beater with a black marijuana leaf printed on the front and jeans that hung around his hips to show off the top of his boxers. A duffel bag was slung over one shoulder.

Carmine could see angular bulges and knew it wasn't full of laundry. More likely guns and ammo. The 9mm he greeted her at the door with was tucked into the front of his jeans.

"Okay, homes, let's go," he said.

Carmine grabbed Ooljee and pulled her to the door. "Sorry again, Graciela," she apologized from the doorway.

"You're welcome, Carmine. And, *cariño*, I'll expect you to come by more often."

Carmine's lips pursed, and then she nodded. That was the price for Rodrigo's help.

Rodrigo bent and gave his mother a quick kiss on the cheek. "*Hasta luego*, Mama."

"Come back in one piece, *bebé*."

He nodded and they trooped out to Carmine's car. Rodrigo tossed the keys into the air and caught them, showing off for Carmine's discomfort. Without hesitation, he headed for the driver's side and unlocked the door.

Carmine forced herself to walk around to the passenger side.

Ooljee hovered, ready to take shotgun when Rodrigo opened the door. Carmine shoved her aside.

"Awwwww," Ooljee whined.

Carmine glared at her until the girl was silent. No way was she riding in the backseat of her own car. And no way in hell was she riding in the back so Ooljee could play house with Rodrigo.

Rodrigo yanked open the door and got in. He started the car and grinned at the roar of the old Detroit engine.

CHaPtER 6

Where are we going?" Carmine asked as Rodrigo pulled away from the curb.

"*Mi hermano* Manny's," Rodrigo said and took the next left. Since Rodrigo didn't have a brother named Manny he must mean gang brother. "Hey, either of you know how to use a gun?" Rodrigo turned to look at Ooljee

"Eyes on the road," Carmine said.

Bad enough Rodrigo took her car but she'd kill him if he wrapped her baby around a lamppost.

"You know how to shoot, cuz?" Rodrigo started unzipping the duffel bag beside him with one hand.

"A little," Carmine said. She didn't like guns and trusted her fists more.

Rodrigo leered over his shoulder. "And you, kitten?"

"I can do okay with the rifle or shotgun. Maybe a revolver."

Carmine cocked an eyebrow but didn't turn around.

Apparently, Rodrigo had the same thought. He said, "Where'd you learn to shoot?"

"On the reservation, guarding our sheep from coyotes."

"Like real ones or shifters?" He watched her in the rear view mirror.

"Plain old coyotes."

Rodrigo dug in his duffel bag, pulled out a pump action sawed-off shotgun, and handed it over the back seat.

"Nice, got shells?"

Ooljee handled the shotgun with apparent ease but Carmine knew the recoil on those things.

She wasn't convinced the skinny bobcat wouldn't end up flat on her ass with the first shot.

With a flourish, Rodrigo produced a box of shotgun shells. Carmine smelled the weedy floral scent of wolfs bane. She watched the box as he tossed it over his shoulder.

"Those are treated, aren't they?"

"Wolf killers," he said. "My own recipe."

A sour taste flooded Carmine's mouth. "And how goes the drug peddling?"

"I'm not the one showing up on your doorstep at 2 a.m., smelling like blood, with Yakuza on my ass, am I?" Rodrigo snapped. "So yeah, the drug peddling is going pretty fucking great, *puta*."

Carmine fell silent. The only sound was the click of Ooljee loading shells into the shotgun breach. She didn't even mean the dig about the drug dealing, but around her family she just couldn't seem to keep her mouth shut. As if by her pointing out the error of their ways, they'd mend them.

"I'm doing you a pretty goddamn big favor," Rodrigo went on, his voice harsh with anger. "We haven't even seen you in two years, not since Angela's *quinceañera*. You don't even call. And now you have the nerve to judge me when I'm all the help you've got?"

"It just slipped out," Carmine said.

"That doesn't sound like 'I'm sorry, Rodrigo,' 'thank you so much, Rodrigo,' 'I'll keep my big fat mouth shut, Rodrigo' to me," he said.

"Oh my God, stop fighting," Ooljee said, emphasizing her words with the pump on the shotgun. "If you want to blame someone, blame me! I got Carmine into this."

"No one's blaming you," Rodrigo said.

"This is family stu—"

A massive impact rocked the Ford, driving it off the road. Glass shattered, raining down on them. Ooljee screamed and bounced off the ceiling of the Galaxie.

Rodrigo smashed into Carmine, knocking her into the passenger side door with enough force to make her bones vibrate.

The car jumped the curb and plowed into a boarded up liquor store. Brick on metal squealed so loud, Ooljee's scream was drowned out.

There was a split second of quiet and Carmine looked around. She thought Rodrigo's bad driving had wrecked them.

But no.

Outside the driver's side window, she saw a black SUV, headlights off, grill crushed against the car door.

"Fuck, it's them!"

Carmine pushed Rodrigo off her. She heard him grunt and saw a smear of blood across his forehead.

He didn't say anything, just grabbed the duffel bag and pulled his 9mm out of his pants.

He opened fire on the SUV and Carmine went deaf from the gunshots. The headlights blazed a second before he shot them out. The SUV reversed course, backing up half a block, either to ram them again or give the occupants a better angle to return fire.

Carmine tried her door but it was stuck shut.

"We have to get out of here," she screamed, distantly noting the touch of hysteria in her voice.

"The windows." Rodrigo was pulling on her jeans, trying to hoist her out of the window himself.

The SUV's flood lamps came on as Carmine was halfway out the window.

Gunshots rang out—dim popping sounds Carmine could barely make out over the ringing in her ears.

The bullets buried themselves in the upholstery of the Ford and pinged off the steel in deadly ricochets.

Carmine hit the glass-covered pavement and pulled Rodrigo out after her.

The Yakuza's rapid fire sounded like hail on a tin roof. The Galaxie absorbed the brunt of the attack and Carmine was grateful to the old gas hog.

"Ooljee?" Carmine screamed in Rodrigo's ear. She guessed he was as deaf as she was.

"On the floor in the back," he shouted, busy with the duffel bag.

He pulled out two small submachine guns and Carmine recognized the profile of an Uzi. A headline maker in the late eighties, the gun had faded from gangster style, replaced by the AK-47 and then the M4.

Rodrigo snapped two overlong clips into place, flicked the safety off with his thumb, and crawled past Carmine.

He fired two short controlled bursts at the SUV, at last interrupting their fire.

"Get Ooljee," he shouted.

Carmine nodded and pulled open the back door. She expected the door to be sticky and almost ripped it off its hinges when it opened smoothly.

Ooljee was on the floor of the back seat, face down, arm twisted across the seat, shotgun still in her hand.

Carmine felt Ooljee's skull and neck bones for breaks.

Nothing—not that she was a doctor, but years of boxing had given her a good knowledge of first aid.

She hauled Ooljee out by the shoulders. Even as dead weight, the bobcat hardly weighed anything. She flipped Ooljee over and shouted, "Wake up!" into her ear.

Blood from a gash on the back of Ooljee's head soaked the pavement and half her face was swelling. But the bobcat stirred, eyes fluttering under lids already turning purple and red.

"Come on! We have to move," Carmine screamed over the gunfire and her own numb eardrums.

Rodrigo ducked back behind the car. "Carmine, grenades."

"What?" No way could she have heard him right.

"We're pinned." He changed the Uzi's clip and pulled a bandolier of grenades from the duffel bag.

"Are you shitting me?"

Rodrigo shook his head. "They have silver slivers in them."

More wolf killers. Carmine took a grenade from the bandolier. The knubby, khaki egg of the grenade was heavier than it looked.

They must have cost a fortune and there were half a dozen on the bandolier.

"What if this silver hits you, too?" she asked between bursts of machine gun fire.

Two of the floodlights on the SUV shattered.

"It's that or we die here," Rodrigo shouted back.

Carmine gripped the grenade, the absurdity of the situation lighting her mind like a firework and cutting through the noise and confusion.

She could almost laugh. "Take Ooljee and go."

Rodrigo looked at her and fired blind. "What?"

"Take Ooljee—"

"I got that. Why?"

"I have a charm for protection against silver. These guys are just human thugs. I can take them."

Rodrigo didn't answer. He pursed his lips and fired over the hood. Then he pulled back.

"All right."

Carmine grabbed a second grenade from the bandolier, just in case she needed a second chance, and put the rest back in the duffel bag.

Crawling, Rodrigo made his way to Ooljee. He slung the duffel bag over one shoulder and patted Ooljee on the cheek. Her eyes were open but unfocused.

"Come on, kitten, time to move."

He helped her sit up. Even seated, she swayed but she managed to stay upright.

Carmine pulled the pin on the first grenade, careful to hold the handle in place.

Her palms were slippery with sweat but she dared not let go.

She looked at Rodrigo and he nodded.

At the first break in fire, Carmine sprang up. She threw the grenade with perfect, major-league-baseball form. A skill gained from having a big backyard and a lot of time on her hands.

The grenade flew straight into the SUV, its windshield long since shot out.

Carmine dropped. She nudged the wolf inside her and it roared to the fore, eager to fight. Her clothes tore at the seams and she was glad she never wore anything too nice to the fights. She toed off the cowboy boots before her back paws could get stuck.

The change also tore open the nearly two hundred stitches in her back. Her snarl of pain was swallowed by the explosion of the grenade.

The roar of fire and screaming metal pierced even her dulled hearing.

Rodrigo was ready. He took off, half dragging, half carrying Ooljee, forcing her staggered steps into a dead run.

Carmine jumped over the roof of the ruined Galaxie and covered half the ground to the SUV in one leap.

She hated to rely on sight alone to locate the Yakuza thugs but it was just about all she had left, with her hearing gone and the overwhelming smell of gunpowder and smoking plastic screwing up her nose.

Two guys were on the ground, burnt and bloody, one on either side of the SUV. They didn't look like much of a threat so she passed them.

There. Two more thugs, one was on the street, trying to crawl away, and one was miraculously halfway down the block already.

Instinct pushed her toward the running target. Carmine loped after him on all fours.

The thug looked over his shoulder and screamed something in Japanese that she couldn't have understood even if her hearing had been intact.

As he ran, he pulled something from his tattered suit jacket. A slightly curved short sword that flashed silver in the streetlights.

Time to put Sejal's charm to the test.

Carmine bore down on her prey, easily closing the distance. There was no way he could outrun her and he knew it.

He turned, sword held out.

The thug made a few slashes with the short sword.

"It's silver, werewolf!" he yelled.

Silver or not, he still had to get within arm's reach to use it against her. The adrenal stink of fear hit Carmine like a wall.

She drooled. The wolf inside her saw meat on two legs, already tenderized.

The confident veneer the Yakuza wore over his terror cracked.

His eyes went wide, even as he assumed a kendo stance she recognized, the sword held over one shoulder like a baseball bat.

Carmine didn't break stride as she reached him. She saw him tense and reared up as he swung.

The short sword grazed her chest, leaving a stinging razor-thin line of blood.

Even a shallow cut from a silver blade should have dropped her like a brick.

The Yakuza's eyes flicked from the blade to her and she saw all rational thought wink out.

His body was way ahead of him and the ammonia stink of piss announced his defeat.

She swiped her massive, clawed hand at the thug's face and tore his head off. A hot fountain of blood spurted from the stump. His body hit the pavement. The head bounced then landed fifteen feet away.

Carmine licked the blood off her muzzle and went back to finish off the other survivor.

The crawler was still struggling to get away. He'd made decent headway, too.

She found him almost twenty feet from the flaming hulk of the SUV.

He shouted and swore at her in angry Japanese as she closed in. He pulled himself over the asphalt, clutching a sheathed short sword the exact copy of Headless Guy's.

Struggling up on his ruined legs, he tried to run for it.

Considering the snail trail of blood he'd left behind, he must have known it was a lost cause. Crawling Guy gave up as Carmine approached.

He rolled over and unsheathed his short sword. Another torrent of Japanese assailed her as he waved the sword in her face.

Her ears swiveled forward trying to pick up his words better. She thought she made out the word "Okami" but that was all she got.

Unlike Headless Guy, Crawling Guy didn't seem like he was going to spit out anything in English any time soon.

Grabbing his arm as he made a swing with the sword, she twisted and pulled, wrenching his arm out of the socket then ripping it off.

His words broke into screaming as arterial blood sprayed across the tarmac.

Too late, Carmine saw the glint of metal in his left hand as she tossed aside the severed arm.

The Yakuza unloaded nearly a full clip into her chest before he bled out.

Shot after shot tore through her body. Searing pain unlike anything she'd felt before burned through her like a hot poker, stabbing into her vitals. She felt as if she were on fire from the inside out.

The force of the gunshots knocked her to the pavement. She writhed and howled, claws raking the ground.

The bullets were silver. She could feel it, like acid in her veins. But it wasn't eating into her tissues, breaking down the cell walls and liquefying her. Sejal's charm worked. Carmine felt it holding the silver at bay. A cold, squirming sensation surrounded the burning balls of silver lodged in her heart, lungs, and stomach.

Carmine prayed to die or pass out but neither happened. The pain went on and on, receding in waves as the charm and her body worked.

An eternity of pain later, she heard a metallic clink. She managed to lift her head and saw a flattened silver slug push slowly out of the wound in her chest.

Amazingly, each bullet, in turn, made its exit. She was disgusted but too fascinated to turn away. It was like watching the surgical shows on TV.

Her own special episode of *Bizarre ER*—nine mangled bullets squeezed out of her flesh.

After the last, she lay on the street, panting hard. She had to get moving.

The four dead guys were only the first wave of thugs.

How many men did the Okami have at his disposal?

She could feel the deep ache of her wounds healing.

With as much damage as the bullets had done, she'd need days to heal. Two or three at least.

But she had to keep moving.

More Yakuza were on their way, coming after Ooljee and Rodrigo.

Carmine rolled over with agonizing slowness, igniting a burst of fire in her chest. She got onto all fours and started walking.

Every movement sent needles of pain through her chest but she kept going.

She went back to the wreck of the Ford and sniffed out Ooljee and Rodrigo's trail. They had headed around back of the liquor store, squeezing through a narrow gap between the store and its derelict neighbor.

Carmine looked over at her Ford Galaxie and the broken bodies near the smoldering SUV.

She couldn't leave her car. Her license and registration in the glove box would take the cops straight to her door.

So could the custom paint job, if they were really on the ball.

Carmine pried the crumpled license plates off the front and back bumpers. She could ditch the plates on the way to catch up with Rodrigo and Ooljee.

Spying the second grenade on the sidewalk where she left it, she snorted a growl and picked it up—carefully. Her paw hand engulfed the grenade, claws clicking on the metal.

Even though she knew she had to get going, she was still loathe to leave the Ford. The gas hog had saved their lives tonight and torching it seemed like such a waste. But ending up in prison would be an even bigger waste.

Carmine got to the corner. She pulled the pin on the grenade.

Luckily, her windshield was gone. She threw the grenade, watching long enough to make sure it landed inside the car.

Then she ducked behind the building on the corner. A few seconds later, she heard the whoosh of the grenade blowing up her car. Carmine gingerly touched the wounds on her chest. The thick black fur around it was sticky and stiff with drying blood. Sejal had better know what she was doing.

She'd promised to dispose of the Yakuza when she could. The question was could she do it in time?

Carmine was too big to take Rodrigo's shortcut between the buildings, so she sniffed around behind them. Rodrigo and Ooljee's trail left the alley and turned right, away from the wreck.

Their scents were easy to follow, made sharper by the adrenaline and blood. Nose to the ground, ears perked, Carmine tracked them.

She had no idea how long she'd been down but the trail hadn't faded. Not that it would. She could have tracked them days from now with her sharp nose.

Every block, Carmine had to pause and rest. If she could have, she'd have lain down among the trash heaps in one of the empty lots she passed.

All she wanted was to sleep. Her body ached with every step and her vision was bleary with fatigue. Instead, she tossed in the license plates and kept walking.

The trail kept going, too, and some half an hour later, by her best guess, she turned a corner and was surprised by what must be her destination.

Kitty-corner from her was an auto repair shop. A faded sign over the metal doors read *Manny's Auto Body: All Makes and Models*. She ran her nose over the ground. That had to be were Rodrigo and Ooljee were. Not just because their scents were still strong, but also because she honestly couldn't go any farther.

She started forward—ears alert for the sound of an approaching vehicle—crossed the street, and examined the garage.

It was quiet. Her eyes darted to the roofline, scanning for movement.

Nothing. Even if there was a trap, she didn't have the energy to run or fight. She edged up to the front door of the garage.

There were only a couple of narrow windows in the solid-brick façade and a mirror over the door so that whoever was inside the shop could see who was on the doorstep. She knocked softly, hoping to not be met with another Yakuza's silver-plated blade.

The door opened and a freckled, pale-tan face peered out.

"Shit, you're as big as Rodrigo said, *chica*."

He must be Manny from the sign. He was a short guy with red hair and made up for his stature with muscle mass. His bulk filled the doorframe but Carmine didn't smell any steroids.

He stepped aside. "Get in."

Panting, Carmine staggered in and sagged forward. Manny caught her. "Damn."

He grunted under the weight and Carmine straightened as best she could.

Rodrigo appeared from the darkened machine shop, rifle ready. As he saw her, he slung it over his shoulder.

"Hurry up, homes," Manny said. "She smells like blood and weighs a ton."

"Goddamn, Carmine, where you been?" Rodrigo asked and rushed to help Manny.

Together they guided her around a greasy front counter and displays of fan belts.

She tripped over a stack of tires and went down hard.

She heard Rodrigo swearing in the background and Manny's face swam in front of her, wavering as little bright spots swarmed across her vision.

"Relax, *chica*, the cavalry's on its way."

CHaPtER 7

Voices woke Carmine—the familiar ones of Rodrigo and Manny and two more she didn't recognize.

Something touched her shoulder and she growled, snapping at whatever it was.

"Geez!" Ooljee yelped. "You almost took my hand off."

The bobcat was kneeling beside Carmine.

There was a big pink Band-Aid stuck to Ooljee's forehead that didn't begin to cover the swollen bump underneath.

Carmine lay on a pile of coveralls that smelled of

motor oil and lube. She wrinkled her muzzle in disgust and got on all fours to shake herself off.

"She's up," Ooljee called out.

"Welcome back," Rodrigo said. He tossed a pair of stained jeans and a T-shirt with the Pennzoil logo on it at her. "Change back, we need to talk."

She picked the clothes off the concrete floor, stood up, and ran a hand over her chest, feeling the nine raised round scars hidden beneath her dense black fur. They were still tender to the touch.

Manny broke away from a muted discussion with two other men. "Come on, there's a storeroom you can change in."

He led her to the back of the garage. There were a couple of doors with peeling gray paint and dark stains. From the left-hand door came a smell of mold, feces, and air freshener.

He pointed at the door and grinned. "You could change in the bathroom but you're too damn big." Manny opened the right-hand door for her. "You'll have to make do with the storeroom, *chica*."

Grateful again for her size advantage, Carmine wrinkled her muzzle at the bathroom.

Judging from smell alone, the bathroom was no place she wanted to be. The storeroom was lit with a bare, sixty-watt bulb that illuminated metal wire racks full of cardboard boxes.

There was enough room for her to squeeze between the shelves but her shoulders brushed the racks on either side.

The door shut behind her and Carmine was glad of a moment's peace. This night couldn't last forever and she just wanted to get to the other end in one piece.

The shift back to human was excruciating. Normally it was a twinge, but her healing wounds tore open then sealed closed as her flesh shrank.

The price for all the shifting in one night was deep and ugly raised scars that took years to fade. If she hadn't had to shift to fight the Yakuza, the scratches on her back that Okami bitch had left would have been gone in a couple days.

Thanks to Doc Herman's stitching, her flesh would've been as smooth and brown as if it'd never happened.

She looked down at her chest. The nine bullet holes stood out, fleshy, roundish scars, thick and pale, dotted her torso.

The highest bullet had just missed her heart and was right over her left breast. The others clustered around her sternum and one wild shot was just under her right breast.

That little Yakuza fucker could shoot. No doubt her back looked just as good. She reached behind her back and felt the Braille of long scars crisscrossing her flesh.

Carmine pulled on the grease-stained jeans and wondered where Rodrigo got them.

They were men's jeans and fit her badly. Too tight at the hips, loose in the crotch and about four inches too short in the pant leg.

Her underwear was gone, too. Her cotton panties and bra had shredded with her other clothes when she first shifted.

Gone just like her snakeskin boots. Her *favorite* pair of snakeskin boots.

She sighed and put on the T-shirt. At least she wasn't naked and, in human form, she could find out what the hell was going on.

Stepping out of the storeroom, Carmine found herself the center of attention. Ooljee and Rodrigo stood close together and the others, Manny and the two gangbangers she'd heard, leaned against a dusty counter.

"Damn, *chica*, you don't get much shorter do you?"

Manny looked her over a little too appraisingly. Perhaps sizing her up for a potential date. He looked disappointed.

Short men were always insecure about tall women. Even barefoot, Carmine towered over him.

Luckily for her. It saved Carmine from shooting him down. She didn't have a lot of dating rules but she maintained a strict no gangsters policy.

"I can't believe you torched the car," Rodrigo said.

"What? How do you know?" Carmine asked.

"Meet Beto and Paco, our resident scrubbers." Rodrigo pointed to the two new guys.

Beto and Paco were a matched set, identical twins styled slightly differently.

Beto had a trimmed goatee, a bandanna headband pulled almost completely over his eyes, and spiky black hair.

Paco kept his hair long, pulled back in a slick ponytail.

No bandanna for him either. Instead, he had half a dozen studs piercing his eyebrows.

The brothers gave Carmine a salute and a grunt, their gazes far more respectful than Manny's.

It might have been because they were human. Shifter gangs had mixed members but the shifters were always the elite.

"You covered our scents then?" Carmine asked.

The brothers grinned at each other.

"Covered," Paco said.

"Erased." Beto said.

"Good work on the car, too," Paco told her.

"No sniffer will find you. Guaranteed." Beto flashed her a few complicated hand gestures that probably meant something then fist bumped Paco.

The LAPD and, in fact, any police department in a city with the budget employed sniffers. Shape-shifting detectives who literally sniffed around crime scenes and caught culprits by scent.

Organized crime and well-prepared perps used chemical scrubbers to eradicate any odors in a fifty-foot radius. The legal limit of a scent conviction. Outside the circle, any smell was just a passerby.

"How long was I out?" she asked.

"Half an hour," Rodrigo told her. "But that's not the problem. Your friends have arrived."

Carmine frowned. She didn't need more bad news.

Ooljee stepped forward. "The Yakuza Shinto priest put a ward around us. No one can get in. Not anyone they don't want, anyway."

"So it's just us five?"

Five against an army. She wished it wasn't true. Wished the Yakuza would just send a couple guys But that would be too much to expect on a night like this.

"Six," Ooljee corrected. "I'm not totally useless."

Carmine snorted. She'd believe it when she saw it. "Can you break the ward?"

"No," Ooljee said. "But I can aim a gun."

"Can I talk to you in private?"

Carmine grabbed Ooljee by the arm and dragged her out of the shop section of the garage and through a connecting door to the auto shop. They didn't stop until they reached the far corner past the last of three hydraulic car lifts.

"Did you tell them about Sejal?" she whispered into Ooljee's ear.

With two pairs of sharp ears back in the shop, Carmine couldn't be too careful.

"Nooo, no, no," Ooljee whispered back. "She likes to keep a low profile."

"Can she break the ward?"

"No problem. We just have to be alive when she gets here."

"She knows where we are? Have you called her?"

"No," Ooljee whispered. She pursed her lips and looked guilty a second. Carmine was about to see if she could beat an answer out of Ooljee but then the skinwalker said, "She knows where I am. Our whole clan has a blood pact with her."

"So we wait." Carmine sighed and rubbed a hand over her face. "Okay."

She hadn't known Ooljee very long but she had the impression that this was about as helpful as she got.

They went back to the grimy shop, Carmine's hope for a quick resolution dashed.

"We got weapons?" she asked.

"And how," Manny said.

"Why aren't they out?"

Rodrigo laughed. "Damn, cuz, you got a plan to pull our asses from the fire?"

She shrugged. "Don't you?"

"Damn straight. But just for fun, let's hear yours."

"Paco and Beto take the roof. We hold the shop."

"Not bad," Rodrigo said, even if his tone was less than congratulatory.

"Why aren't we taking positions?" Carmine asked.

She stepped up to Rodrigo, using every inch of her six-foot-three-inch height to get in his face. She could feel anger coming off him. The tension in his muscles said he wanted to punch her but didn't dare.

He was the big bad gangster. He was the one who was supposed to be making the decisions. That was the entire reason she had come to him in the first place.

So far all he had done was flirt with Ooljee and leave her to get shot in the chest nine times.

"You woke up and distracted us," he said.

He stared unblinking into her eyes. An obvious challenge she wished she had the time to take him up on.

"It's cool though," Manny interrupted.

He held up his hands. Trying for a friendly peace-keeping maneuver, he squeezed between Carmine and Rodrigo, forcing them back a few steps.

They both glared at him, eyes narrow and Carmine's lip curled.

Manny didn't move, though. "Ooljee said the ward only went up fifteen minutes ago. She can sense it. Part of her skin-walker powers or something."

"Get the guns," Carmine said. "I'm taking point."

"You? What the hell?" Rodrigo asked.

"I've got the charm against silver." Carmine turned to Manny. "You got a stash here?"

"Course." He smirked, a feral glint lit his dark brown eyes. "Paco, Beto, come on."

He jerked his head in the direction of the bathroom. They followed him to the back of the shop.

Curious to see the stash, Carmine went after them. Rodrigo tugged her arm, trying to stop her.

She pulled her arm out of his grip with a bit more difficulty than she expected. "What?"

He grabbed her again and tried to swing her around to face him.

Carmine planted her feet and refused to budge until he let go.

Rodrigo relented and Carmine turned to him.

"I thought you were dead," he said, his voice almost inaudible. He glanced at the others, crowded around the bathroom door. "When it took you so long to get here—"

Carmine choked back an automatic snide reply. She could see the concern in his eyes.

She was surprised and then ashamed to be surprised. He was her blood, after all. They'd grown up together.

"I told you about the charm," she said again.

His concern made her uncomfortable. It messed with the image she had of him as a psycho gang banger and reminded her that she was the one who'd quit on her family, not Rodrigo.

"Come on, how often do those things ever work?" he said to the floor.

He'd done that since they were kids. Any time he was embarrassed, he stared at the ground.

"You were worried." She hadn't meant to say that out loud.

"Bitch, of course I was."

He looked at her square in the eyes, challenging her to say something nasty or weakly sentimental.

"Don't worry. I'm pretty goddamned hard to kill."

Rodrigo nodded. "If you ever wanted a career change, the Lobo Reyes could use you."

She grinned. "I think marketing is dangerous enough."

"Hey, come get your guns," Manny called to them.

He stood in the doorway of the bathroom, handing an enormous assault rifle to Paco.

Carmine cocked her head and looked over Manny's shoulder. All she could see was blank brick wall through the bathroom door. "Where is he getting those?"

Rodrigo gently punched her arm. "Come on, I'll show you."

She followed him to the bathroom and covered her nose. Not that it helped. Did they ever bother to clean it? Of course, that smell would throw off drug-sniffing shifters so there was probably good reason for the stink.

Just as Manny had said, it was too small for her werewolf form. Her closets at home were bigger.

There was a small toilet with a chipped black seat in one corner and a triangular sink wedged in beside the door.

A portion of the tiled wall behind the toilet had been removed, revealing a sizable cubbyhole.

"So what's your poison?" Manny asked.

He knelt on the toilet lid, waiting for her answer.

"None of them," she said.

He winked. "Shotgun it is."

"Another sawed-off," Carmine said as she took it.

She never used guns and this was her second in one night.

She hated them. Simple killing machines that put death in the hands of any fool willing to do some damage.

Guns had no discretion, no thought, killing anyone in their path. Children, civilians, anyone. It was lazy and arbitrary.

The way she fought, there were no accidents. No bystanders. All parties involved knew what they were getting into.

"Maximum spread that way. Just aim in the general direction of your target. You'll hit something."

She nodded but still felt uncomfortable. Her stomach clenched with hunger and fear.

She wasn't sure which was worse, the anticipation or the actual battle.

Manny poked her with a cardboard box. "Box of shells."

Carmine looked down at the box stupidly. There was a label on top but all it had was numbers. Presumably, they meant something but it may as well have been Greek.

"You load them into the breach and they're ejected each time you fire. Keep the box with you so you can reload," Manny told her.

"Just take the fucking box," Rodrigo said.

Carmine ignored him. "Are they silver?"

"No. Ooljee said it would be mostly humans coming."

"Good." She took the box. "Got anything to eat?"

"Behind the counter," Manny said.

Hungry didn't begin to describe the gnawing pit in her stomach. She'd shifted four times in one night, won a prizefight against an Okami, and survived a gun battle. If she didn't eat something soon, she'd be eating one of them. She elbowed her cousin aside and headed for the counter to eat and try loading the shotgun.

Paco and Beto were there, magazines for their assault rifles neatly laid out beside the cash register. Carmine put down the shotgun and looked for the promised food.

A few dozen kinds of jerky hung on the wall. Beef jerky, pepperoni sticks, and even turkey jerky. Good enough.

Carmine started at the top and grabbed a handful of packets. She tore the first one open with her teeth and emptied the entire leathery contents into her mouth. She chewed the peppery beef, trying to maneuver it with her tongue so it didn't stab the roof of her mouth.

When the mass of jerky was soft, she swallowed and tore open another packet.

As busy as Paco and Beto were, they both stopped to watch her eat.

Most shifters could eat voraciously but werewolves were almost in a class by themselves. The entire wall of jerky amounted to little more than a light snack.

"There's some energy drinks under the counter," Paco ventured.

Mouth full, Carmine nodded a thanks for the heads up and ducked down to look.

Sure enough, there was a little cooler with a sliding glass door stocked with Red Bull, Rock Star, and Monster energy drinks.

She grabbed a monster can of Monster and washed

down the beef jerky with the sticky, sweet, chemical-tasting drink.

In between packets of jerky and cans of energy drinks, Carmine loaded shells into the shotgun.

Beto showed her how to do it after she almost loaded the first shell backward. He also told her that, contrary to movie myth, she didn't actually have to pump the shotgun after each fire.

The shotgun automatically loaded the next round after each shell was ejected.

Paco and Beto finished up and took their assault rifles and ammo to the roof.

There was an access hatch in a corner of the machine shop where Carmine and Ooljee had conferenced earlier.

A second after they left, Rodrigo, Manny, and Ooljee came to the counter with the rest of the munitions. She looked at the number and kind of the guns.

"Jesus, waiting for the apocalypse?" she asked around the pepperoni stick she was gnawing.

Manny winked at her. "I like to be prepared." He eyed the piles of empty jerky packets and crushed cans of energy drinks. "You gonna pay for that?"

Carmine swept them off the counter to make room for a dozen or so guns and twice as many boxes of ammo. "Bill me."

The amount of firepower Manny had just put down

seemed extraordinary for a street gang. Even with her minimal knowledge of guns.

She gave the shop a second look. The machine shop must be a cover. They probably ran drugs through here. Stored them. Moved great big, multi-thousand-dollar blocks of Mexico's finest heroin through it.

"That's why there's roof access and why the windows are so small. It's to withstand a police assault."

"Got it in one," Rodrigo said with only token sarcasm.

He was busy with his own weaponry. An assault rifle and more oversized clips for his antique Uzis.

"I'm not complaining," Ooljee said as she expertly loaded a sleek but compact rifle that Carmine didn't recognize.

"I know you're not, kitten," he said and gave her shoulder a squeeze.

Carmine rolled her eyes. As Klaus would say, she'd performed a mitzvah tonight.

Introducing her cousin to Ooljee, her only hope was not to be invited to the wedding.

Then a second thought struck her cold. If Ooljee and Rodrigo did hook up, Ooljee could tell him about her real job as a pit fighter.

She'd rather risk Sejal's wrath and let Ooljee die.

The pepperoni stick turned to sand in her mouth and she spat it out.

Ooljee shivered and her eyes went wide, filming over with gold. She clutched the barrel of the rifle and Carmine could see her shaking.

"The ward's been breached."

"Is it down?" Carmine asked.

Maybe Sejal had come. An adrenal surge of hope made the hair on the back of her neck stand up.

"No, it just went down for a second. They're here."

Rodrigo shoved Ooljee toward the machine shop. "Get up to the roof."

Ooljee refused to budge. "What? I can be more use down here."

"It's safer up there," Rodrigo shouted.

He pushed her again, hard and Ooljee stumbled. Still the bobcat hesitated. Her lower lip quivered but her eyes flashed gold and catty with defiance.

Rodrigo made a grab for her, but Ooljee dodged his hand and darted away.

She shot one more rebellious glare over her shoulder before heading for the ladder.

"We could have used her, man," Manny said.

"Shut up," Rodrigo said.

Manny shrugged and took a position under one of the narrow front windows. He used the butt of his gun to smash it.

"Get the other one."

Rodrigo pointed to the window slit farthest from

the door. It was high on the wall above a shelf of boxed car parts.

Copying Manny, Carmine smashed the glass of the window in front of her.

She had to lean on a shelf to point the shotgun out the window and Carmine knew why Rodrigo had put her there.

With her elbow propped on the top of the shelf, she could hold the shotgun perfectly level, a big help for aiming.

A rifle shot cracked the night air. Carmine jumped, panic forcing her heart into overdrive.

She hadn't realized how quiet it was or how on edge she was. She was starting to regret the ball of beef jerky in her stomach.

Even though the window was narrow, Carmine still had a decent field of vision.

The garage was on the corner and she could see the cross street as well as the street in front of her. That didn't mean she liked the view.

Five SUVs were converging on the garage. All in uniform black, varying in model from an ostentatious Hummer to pimped out Escalades.

Another rifle shot rang out, even louder than before, and Carmine saw a deep scratch appear in the paint job of the Hummer. Her lip curled. The vision of her Swiss-cheesed Ford rose up in her mind.

The Yakuza, or at the very least their cars, needed to pay.

But judging by the lack of damage, the Yakuza mini fleet was warded and armored. Which meant her Ford would go un-avenged. God forbid anything could be easy.

Paco or Beto, or maybe Ooljee, shot the other cars once each to test the armor. Then there was nothing.

Carmine's hand sweated on the trigger of the shotgun. She looked at Rodrigo, calm and grim as he knelt beside the door.

"Do we fire?" she asked, fighting to keep her voice level.

"Wait till they get out of the cars," he told her.

"But what if they don't?"

"They will, don't worry," Manny said.

Her attention returned to the window. Rodrigo and Manny seemed to know something she didn't. Not that they had decided to fill her in.

All she could do was wait for the order to fire, like the buck private in a war movie. She pushed aside her anger. This was why she'd come to Rodrigo.

He had better know what he was doing or they were all toast.

From the corner of her eye, Carmine saw something fly at the Hummer. There was a metallic thunk as it hit the roof and bounced off.

Another grenade. Carmine ducked behind the shelves and braced herself. Manny and Rodrigo put their backs to the wall.

The explosion roared, the blast shaking the garage. Two more followed and she felt the concussion vibrate in her bones. Her ears went numb for a second time that night.

She waited for another explosion, but what felt like minutes ticked by with nothing happening. Though judging by the double-time beat of her heart, she'd only been waiting seconds.

A glow in the corner of her eye caught her attention. Manny was texting one-handed, thumb flying over the tiny keys of his cell phone.

"Are you shitting me? Can't it wait?" She could hear her own voice distantly which meant her eardrums were mending.

"It's Paco, you idiot," Rodrigo snapped. "He's reporting in."

Manny frowned at the phone and then looked out the skinny window. "Dammit," he snarled.

His ears grew pointy and Carmine could see him pale under his freckles.

Carmine couldn't resist a peek and neither could Rodrigo. They both checked their windows.

"Fuck," she whispered.

The SUVs had indeed been abandoned. Some

twenty gun- and blade-wielding thugs hovered behind a man in a white robe.

Five paper charms hung in a pentacle formation in front of Robed Guy.

Carmine could see the glowing red force lines of magic connecting each charm.

"The Shinto priest," she breathed.

Ooljee had warned her but even being prepared didn't make his little magic show any less impressive. How were they going to break that ward? It completely shielded the Yakuza.

Cool night air brought a dozen scents to her nose. Carmine inhaled deeply, sucking air through her nose and mouth to get the full taste of the odors.

The ozone smell of magic, silver from the Yakuza swords, human fear, sweat, and excitement. More telling was the musky wolf smell of the Okami Boss from Sejal's waiting room.

Boss Okami's daughter wasn't with him. She was probably still reeling from the head trauma Carmine had inflicted.

The one thing a shifter couldn't bounce back from quickly was brain damage. Though unlike a human, she'd still come back from it intact.

Another shot fired from above broke the silence. Carmine wasn't the only one who flinched.

Most of the thugs dropped to a crouch. All except

the most confident and their Shinto priest. The thugs didn't have to worry. The ward lit up as the bullet ricocheted off.

Now what?

Sit here and wait to die?

Carmine stared at Rodrigo. He was still and patient, his face set in harsh determination.

He wasn't even sweating. Carmine was clammy with it. Sweat dripped down her back and beaded on her forehead.

Guilt mixed heavily with the fear. Maybe she'd made a mistake coming to Rodrigo.

The vision of Graciela crying over their two coffins flashed into her mind.

"I'm sorry," Carmine said. The words popped out. She wasn't even aware of deciding to speak.

"What?" Rodrigo didn't take his eyes off the window.

"I'm sorry I came to you. You wouldn't be here if it wasn't for me. I should have just taken Ooljee and kept driving."

"Are you apologizing because you think we're going to die?"

"Yes."

"Hold that thought," Rodrigo said and pointed out the window.

She looked out the empty pane. The scene had

changed. The Yakuza all had guns in hand aimed at the garage.

Something flashed in the streetlights.

A glass bottle hurled from the roof. It smashed against the ward right in front of the priest's face.

Blackish liquid oozed over the surface of the ward. Holes appeared in the shimmering wall, the glowing edges spreading, eaten away by the contents of the bottle like acid thrown on fabric.

The smell of burning blood singed Carmine's nose. The bottle had held a ward breaker made from blood. Whose blood it was or where the spell came from she didn't want to know.

The priest gestured frantically and the thugs behind him took a step back, eyes widening in fear. But it was already too late.

Carmine heard the shot the same instant she saw the Shinto priest's head explode. The ward blinked out of existence before the body even hit the ground and more shots came from above.

Rodrigo and Manny opened fire.

Any of the Yakuza's foot soldiers not fast enough to duck behind the armored fleet were gunned down.

The street emptied and the gunfire stopped all at once. Silence rang in Carmine's ears.

The paper charms that had hung in the air seconds ago fluttered to the ground like dying birds.

The sudden quiet was so thorough Carmine thought she'd finally gone deaf.

"Why the fuck didn't you fire?" Rodrigo shouted.

Startled Carmine realized he was right. She looked at the shotgun in her hands. Barrel cool, smelling of gun oil instead of cordite.

"Aren't you some bad ass martial artist? Hands of lightning? What the fuck are you doing?"

"Leave her alone," Manny said.

Carmine couldn't think of anything to say. She hadn't frozen, it just hadn't occurred to her to fire.

She'd been so intent on watching what was happening that she just sat there like it was all happening on TV.

This wasn't the combat she was used to. Face-to-face, she looked into her opponent's eyes and saw the gears turning.

She'd always fought and killed that way, as an animal, as a wolf. There was no guilt that way. She remembered them all well enough.

A lot of shifters retained most of their human faculties in animal form, but not guilt. Nature had no remorse and neither did shifters.

Gunning someone down in human form was different.

There was no quick way to explain any of that to Rodrigo.

Carmine was about to tell him she'd fire next time when the shooting began in earnest.

The Yakuza opened fire from behind the line of vehicles. The piercing, sharp retorts echoed in her ears.

This time Carmine fired. There wasn't a human target in sight. She aimed at the SUVs. She doubted the buckshot was even making it across the street.

The intense crossfire lasted seconds, or minutes—Carmine still couldn't tell. Then she was out of shells.

She ducked behind the shelf and pulled more shotgun shells from her pockets.

She reloaded, her hands shaking, slowing her down. It had been years since she'd been this frightened.

A sound from up above startled her. Carmine dropped a shell and swore.

The noise was a cross between an explosion and a whistling firework. She looked out the window and waited for the roof to collapse.

A black Escalade exploded. The fireball searing orange across her retinas.

The Cadillac lifted into the air, clearing the pavement then crashing back into place.

Yakuza scrambled like black-suited cockroaches, seeking shelter behind the other vehicles.

Carmine heard Rodrigo and Manny cheering. "What was that?" she yelled.

"RPG, baby!" Rodrigo told her.

For a second Carmine thought she heard wrong, then she realized she should quit playing Xbox so much. Not role-playing game but rocket propelled grenade.

How a bunch of LA gang bangers got an RPG she didn't want to know.

She was just grateful they had one.

Another rocket screamed overhead and a Subaru went up in a blaze of fire.

Then the Hummer.

Manny and Rodrigo didn't waste any time. They fired on the scattered thugs across the street. She saw the fountains of blood spray as bodies dropped.

Carmine fired randomly any time she saw a shadowed form cross in front of the flames. She didn't seem to hit anything.

Either she was a crap shot or the spread of the buckshot was too thin. Apparently, she was the last line of defense since the Yakuza would have to get a lot closer.

Rodrigo must have figured if that happened it wouldn't matter what kind of gun she had. They'd given her the firepower equivalent of busy work.

The fires died down to glowing flickers and acidic black smoke blanketed the street as the cars' plastics and rubber burned.

She frowned. That wasn't right.

The smoke should be rising but something was keeping it at the street level.

Carmine looked out at the corpse of the Shinto priest. It was still there straddling the centerline.

"Ooljee's wrong," she shouted over the gun blasts. "They have another magic user! Are you listening?"

Rodrigo paused and peered out the window.

The choking black smoke obscured everything, the SUVs, the Yakuza, even the streetlights were gone, swallowed up in hazy darkness.

"Fucking hell, she's right," Rodrigo growled.

"It must be Papi Okami," Carmine said.

As if her words were prophetic, the graying Yakuza boss ghosted out of the smoke. He hurled a flat white object at the machine shop and ghosted out before anyone got a shot off.

An explosion rocked the garage, shaking the plaster from the ceiling and knocking boxes to the floor. Carmine lost her footing and fell over.

A whole section of the shop caved in. Bricks rained down on Manny and Rodrigo in a storm of dust and debris. The building stopped shaking a few seconds later. Carmine coughed out a mouthful of grit and crawled to her feet. Damn sly Okami.

Carmine should have known better. Should have guessed the old man would have something extra up his sleeve even if Ooljee hadn't.

"Rodrigo?" she croaked. "Manny?"

Two messy piles of brick shifted. Rodrigo emerged first, snarling as he pulled himself out of the rubble. He was fighting not to change.

She could see his nails had lengthened to claws and his ears had grown pointed. He held on because werewolf claw hands couldn't fit through a trigger guard.

They were alive. Carmine let out a ragged sigh. She never thought she'd be this happy to see Rodrigo's face in her lifetime.

Manny groaned and staggered upright. A bright red lump showed through the carroty bristle of his hair. Even Manny was a relief to see.

She hardly knew him but he'd helped her out twice already, catching her at the door and coming between her and Rodrigo.

"Are you all right?" Carmine asked, then as they both nodded, her gaze flicked over the rest of the garage.

The front of the auto shop had collapsed and there was a gaping hole torn in the façade.

There were still a dozen or more Yakuza out there, waiting behind the smokescreen.

They had an open invitation with half the wall gone. Without the walls for defense, Carmine and her friends were sitting ducks. The thugs could swarm in any minute.

How many were left in the garage? Carmine was fine. Rodrigo was fine.

Manny was upright, the knot on his head swelling even as she watched.

But the three on the roof, Ooljee, Paco, Beto? What about them? Without their cover fire, they didn't have a chance.

Rodrigo obviously had the same thought. He looked up at the ceiling, shouted, "Hey! Anyone hurt?"

Carmine and Manny followed Rodrigo's gaze. No reply.

"Hey! Anyone?"

Still nothing. They might be dead, or unconscious. Carmine might have failed.

She was worried less about failing Sejal, although the Naga was ever present in the back of her mind, but the worst of it was failing Graciela. Failing herself.

They could all die here, for nothing, and it was her fault.

She raised the shotgun and turned to the hole in the building. "We don't have time for this."

"We should get to the roof," Rodrigo said, ignoring her.

Something white and wispy caught the corner of Carmine's eye. A sick feeling, cold and sinking, squeezed her intestines. She knew what it was even as she turned her head and opened her mouth.

Boss Okami ghosted in, materializing right behind Manny.

Before Carmine could utter a sound, she saw a flash of silver glinting dimly in the darkness.

The sword plunged into Manny's back.

The old wolf ghosted out again before Manny even registered the wound.

"Manny," Carmine yelled, too late.

He looked down at himself, worry wrinkling his brow. His mouth opened to say something but blood bubbled out, spilling down his chin and soaking into his shirt.

"¡*Dios*! ¡*Mierda*!" Rodrigo spun on his heel and raised his gun searching for a target.

Carmine ran to Manny. She caught him just before he hit the ground. Gently as possible, she lowered him to the concrete floor.

The telltale rattle of his lung filling with blood told her everything she needed to know. The blade the Okami had struck with was silver and Manny's lung wasn't just punctured, it was dissolving.

"Manny," Carmine said.

His eyes were losing focus already. He reached out blindly and she took his hand. He tried to grin and managed a grimace. His eyes focused on her for a second and Carmine's heart clenched tight with sorrow. She couldn't quit the refrain that this was all her fault.

All the death and all the violence went straight back to her.

"Don't worry," Manny whispered. Blood boiled from his mouth with every word.

"I'm sorry," Carmine told him.

He coughed or laughed, she couldn't be sure. "Just cry at my funeral, *chica*."

Then nothing.

A final burbling exhale and Manny was gone. She didn't even know his last name.

CHAPTER 8

Rodrigo tugged on her arm but Carmine couldn't move. She felt paralyzed, dizzy, heavy, and light. She felt too much all at once.

"Get up, you great big bitch! He's here," Rodrigo shouted into her ear.

Carmine smelled ozone. Her nose twitched. She was herself again.

The hackles on the back of her neck rose and she stood, turning in the direction of the scent.

Rodrigo turned in a circle firing wildly in the dust and ruins of the demolished shop.

The Okami was ghosting in and out, appearing for

a split second and gone before Rodrigo could aim, wasting Rodrigo's ammo.

"Stop it," Carmine told Rodrigo.

She tried to grab his shoulder but he spun away from her, trying to anticipate where the Okami would appear next.

He wasn't listening and it didn't look like he was going to start, even though he knew she knew how to fight them.

On the next turn, Carmine ducked the rifle and came up low.

She shoved Rodrigo hard, putting her whole body into it.

He careened toward the shop wall and crashed into some half-collapsed shelves, pulling them down as he hit the floor.

He glared at her. "What the fuck?"

"Get your back to the wall."

Carmine saw his eyes narrow then widen. She knew why when the ozone hit her nose. Now it was her turn to fight.

She dropped to the floor and rolled, even as she heard Rodrigo's inarticulate warning shout.

The Okami's blade whistled over her head, so close she felt the breeze of it passing.

She kicked out blindly and her foot snagged a pant leg.

Not much, but the Okami was forced to shift positions before he could aim another strike.

She regained her feet and sprang up in a fighting stance, feet spread, knees bent, fists up to protect her face.

The old wolf sneered at her. His gray hair stood on end and she saw a hint of fang.

"First you, then your scum, then the bobcat if she isn't dead already," Ishiguro said.

Carmine danced back a few feet, hoping to stay out of sword reach.

"How's your daughter? She wake up yet?"

Ishiguro snarled, and leapt, silver blade arcing through the air. Carmine dodged as he swung. Even angry, his form was perfect.

She'd been hoping to rattle him, make him lose his temper, but his obvious years of practice won out. He was going to slaughter her.

She might have been taking martial arts classes her whole life but so had the old dog and he had a good thirty years of brutal practice on her. She wished she hadn't lost the shotgun. She couldn't even recall dropping it.

A shot rang out, and Carmine saw a chunk of concrete fly up from the floor. Ishiguro froze mid-sword stroke.

"Drop it, you *puto* bitch," Rodrigo said.

Carmine saw he'd listened to her and kept his back to the wall. The assault rifle was trained on Ishiguro.

The crazy old wolf grinned. "Those aren't silver."

"No, but if I put enough into your brain, I bet it won't matter."

"Do it," Carmine yelled. "This isn't a fucking Bond movie! Shoot him!"

Rodrigo pulled the trigger and Carmine heard a click. Jammed or out of bullets it didn't matter, they were still screwed.

"Shit!"

Rodrigo lowered the gun a fraction and Ishiguro pivoted. He swung the sword one-handed at Carmine, just to keep her back, and reached into the breast pocket of his suit with the other. He pulled another slip of paper out.

This time Carmine was close enough to see the glowing writing wriggling across the surface.

"Get down," she screamed at Rodrigo.

He jumped for the counter as the paper charm flew past his head. Ishiguro ghosted out and Carmine took that as a hint to find cover.

She curled up on the floor just as the amulet hit the wall.

The wall lit with a faint red glow then exploded just like the roof had. The explosion rocked the already shaky building.

Carmine felt the blast roll over her like a giant fist but there was no heat.

Chunks of brick pounded her body and she kept her arms over her head.

When the hail of brick was over, she jumped up. The auto shop was unrecognizable.

Two holes gaped in opposite walls. The roof was held up only by the corner support, a now exposed steel beam.

Where had the counter gone? Carmine rubbed her watering eyes and tried to blink away the brick dust. There, a lump of rubble, shattered glass, and the smell of spilled energy drinks. That had to be it.

She took three steps before she caught a whiff of ozone. She spun out with a roundhouse kick and hit home.

Ishiguro grunted and staggered but kept his feet. While he was still off-balance, she kicked again, a solid strike to his wrist. He dropped the sword and Carmine kicked it away.

For half a heartbeat, Carmine thought maybe she had him. Maybe without the sword he wouldn't be so much trouble.

The Okami made a grab for her. His sharp nailed fingers clamped down on her forearm and he yanked, pulling her up and over.

Carmine hit the rubble-studded floor hard, chunks

of brick and scattered car parts dug into her. She felt every injury she'd sustained that night ignite in fresh pain.

The bastard was fast and Carmine wasn't exactly in fighting form. She saw a blur of motion heading for her face and rolled aside. The old man's foot came down where her head had been.

He struck again and she caught his foot and twisted. He went sprawling and ghosted as he hit the ground.

If boss man himself had gone into the ring tonight Carmine might not have walked out.

He was what his daughter would be in another twenty years.

Deadly.

Carmine jumped up into a crouch. She turned her head, trying to look everywhere at once.

He might come from behind like most Okami tended to do.

Or he might surprise her from the front. Or he'd tag her with a paper charm and blow her damn head off.

Carmine's feet went out from under her and, too late, she smelled the ozone. She hit the floor, tucking and rolling. A hard blow caught her chin as she came up and she felt her teeth slam together.

Blood and shards of teeth filled her mouth. Carmine spat them out, her mouth still tasting of iron and dirt.

Her vision went starry and dim but she instinctively pulled away in another tuck and roll.

The retreat bought her the seconds she needed to leap back on her feet.

Ishiguro stood a few feet away, just waiting for her. His breath came out hard but he had tons more stamina than his daughter did.

A lot more arrogance, too. Unfortunately well-earned arrogance. Carmine wiped her hands on her T-shirt, staining it with more blood and sweat.

He rushed her, coming with a fluid series of attacks, probably Chinese in origin.

She desperately blocked each one, losing ground as he drove her back toward the barely standing wall. No doubt, his thugs were outside waiting to see their boss kill her.

Carmine's foot landed in a miniature oil spill where a bottle of Quaker State had smashed. Ishiguro's next blow sent her foot sliding out from under her.

She landed hard and wrong on her knee and felt the tendons rip. A stab of fresh agony exploded in her leg.

He struck, palm flat, aiming for a devastating blow to the nose, which would drive bone chips into her brain.

Carmine jerked her head away at the last instant.

He hit the side of her face and her cheekbone shattered.

Boiling hot pain radiated from the blow and spiked behind her eyes.

She was on the floor, looking up through one eye, unsure how she got there. Carmine was down for the count. How many years had it been?

Above her was the merciless toothy sneer of Ishiguro. Then he disappeared from sight.

Was he stupid? Carmine tried to get up. She still had a chance. Arrogant old fuck. How dare he turn his back on her?

She struggled up to her elbows and a nauseating wave of dizziness spun the room.

Her leg wouldn't work either. She managed to get up briefly but the other leg wouldn't take the weight. The knee she'd gone down on refused to function and she went down hard, her leg twisting painfully to the side.

Carmine bit down on a scream. She didn't have time for the distraction.

Then Ishiguro was back. And she found out why he'd disappeared.

He'd found his sword.

He rested the blade against her neck, taking aim. The razor thin line of the silver blade searing and cold against her flesh.

Then pulled it back.

The blow would be swift if he was good, and Carmine knew he was. He would take her head off in one swipe.

She stared up, vision hazy, her good eye following the path of the sword.

This was it. The end.

She should feel something. Her life should be flashing before her eyes. Instead, she just felt stupid and dull and angry and her face hurt so bad she wished he'd just kill her already.

A silent shadow hit Ishiguro in the side. The Okami flew sideways with a grunt.

Something was on him, something big. He shouted and snarled as he struggled.

Carmine blinked. A furious yowling ball of spotted fur was tearing Ishiguro a new one.

The bobcat, big as a wolfhound, ripped into the Yakuza boss, flesh tearing as easily as the fabric of his Armani suit.

Ooljee. Carmine's aching jaw hung slack. Apparently, the girl was good for something.

Ishiguro finally lost it. His guttural cries turned feral as he shifted into wolf form. He was the same half wolf of most werewolves but his age showed, his pelt had gone gray but the muscles were still taught beneath the skin.

Ooljee hung on with tooth and claw, writhing and twisting out of his reach.

She couldn't hang on forever. Carmine shook herself out of her daze. She needed a weapon.

The samurai sword was a few feet away. Carmine crawled for it on her belly, her useless leg dragging behind her.

She pulled herself on her elbows. Every inch forward sent a throb of red-hot pain through her knee.

Sweating like she'd run a marathon Carmine reached for the sword. The hilt was cool, the sharkskin grip sandpapery under her skin. Now, what to do with it?

"Ooljee! Get him over here!" She hoped Ooljee could still understand her. Carmine bit her lip and got herself into a sitting position.

Ooljee kicked Ishiguro in the muzzle and leapt away. The bobcat's fur was matted with blood and, from the smell, some was hers.

She streaked toward Carmine in a blur of speed, which meant she couldn't be too hurt.

The Okami shook himself and howled in rage. Silver-gray fur spiked up on the back of his neck and he ran after Ooljee who had shot past Carmine and disappeared somewhere behind.

Blinded by anger, Ishiguro stepped in the same puddle of oil Carmine had. His clawed feet scrabbled on the slick floor, his arms swinging wide trying to balance.

It would have been funny at any other time.

The wolf went down face first right beside Carmine. Relief washed over her that he hadn't landed on her.

She swung the sword two-handed, bringing it up over her head. The wolf caught the movement from the corner of his eyes and she saw them widen.

Too late. The sword came down on his neck. The stroke landed but Carmine had no skill and no leverage. It was a messy blow that sliced into the thick meat of his neck.

She pulled the sword away and a jet of blood sprayed her. Carmine hacked again, this time cutting to the bone.

He flailed, body twitching, his growls turning to pathetic gurgles as blood pumped from his artery.

Carmine didn't have time to feel disgusted with him or herself. If he got back up, it was over for her.

She hacked again and again. Taking three more ugly wild blows to chop his head off.

When she finally cut through the spinal cord, Carmine shoved the head away from the body, just in case the wolf could somehow knit his fibers back together.

She heard a high, rhythmic whine in her ears and wondered what it was. Then she realized it was her own breathing. She was panting hard through airways constricted with panic.

Carmine fell back exhausted. Her chest was tight and she couldn't get enough air. She shut her eyes but opened them again when all she saw was the butchery she'd just committed.

Ooljee slunk back, still in bobcat form. Her gold eyes looked down into Carmine's and her tufted ears swiveled in concern. Ooljee bent down and nuzzled Carmine.

"I'll live," Carmine whispered. She tried to push Ooljee away but the bobcat's head snapped up.

Ears going flat, Ooljee hissed at something behind Carmine. She twisted around to see what had set the bobcat off.

Silhouetted in the torn side of the auto shop were a dozen men. Carmine knew who they were even before she heard the rapid-fire cursing in Japanese.

Carmine sagged. She didn't have any fight left.

Rodrigo was buried along the far wall, unconscious if not dead, Manny was growing cold across the room, and only Ooljee knew Paco and Beto's fates. Too bad she couldn't really talk right now.

Ooljee pressed close to Carmine as if that would save her. Warm dense fur wrapped around Carmine. At least she wouldn't die alone.

The Yakuza thugs spread out and picked their way over shattered bricks and tires, loose spark plugs and stray fan belts.

They kept their weapons raised, gun and sword alike.

The bravest of them marched over to his boss's body.

He stood there, jaw tightening with rage, looking down at the Okami's severed head. Then he turned to Carmine and shouted at her in Japanese.

From the vein throbbing in his temple, she got the idea he was pretty pissed off.

"He wants to know how you can dishonor your enemy by butchering him so badly."

Carmine's heart skipped a beat and she looked around, eyes wide with hope. The taste of sandalwood and ozone drifted to her nose.

The hair on her arms stood up as she felt the tingle of magic.

Ooljee yowled, back arching, claws raking the concrete in feline triumph.

Everyone in the shop turned at the sound of the throaty voice.

A long serpentine shadow separated from the ruined wall.

Sejal.

The atmospheric pressure of Sejal's power pressed on the garage. The air thickened and it felt like the minutes before a storm.

In slow motion, the Yakuza swung their guns

around to retrain them on Sejal. But like bugs caught in syrup, they couldn't move fast enough.

Sejal, moving at normal speed, snapped her fingers. A torrent of liquid gold flowed in through the open walls.

Tigers, a dozen of the big cats—maybe more— Carmine couldn't tell. Power, like static electricity, sparked off their striped fur.

There were so many and so big, ten and twelve feet long, that the cats blurred together in a single roaring wall.

They swam through the thickened air like sharks cutting through water. A massive tiger bore down on the Yakuza soldier, who moments ago had been yelling at Carmine.

The cat's jaws yawned wide, showing ivory-yellow fangs longer than her hand.

The thug was standing there one second and gone the next. Head snapped off and swallowed in a single bite, the body disappearing under a freight train of orange and black.

All around the garage the same fate fell on the Yakuza gang. The tigers cut them down where they stood. Not even a single one had the chance to fire.

Then it was over. There was a whoosh as normal time or normal atmospheric pressure reinstated itself. Carmine's ears popped and she yawned to clear them.

Blood mixed on the floor with motor oil and car lube. Each tiger snatched up a body in its huge jaws and carried the carcass out with no more effort than a bird dog fetching a dead duck.

A last huge tiger, tall as a man at the shoulder, silently bore away the body of Ishiguro, leaving the head behind.

Sejal glided over the rubble, quiet as night falling, and stroked the fur of the passing tiger. She settled in front of Carmine and Ooljee, playful confidence showing on her pretty features.

"Safe and sound then?" she asked them.

Carmine shook her head, too numb to speak. Was Sejal that callous? Or did she think she was being funny?

Maybe the cold-blooded snake just got off on the carnage, like an expert chess player sacrificing pieces. Dull rage burned in Carmine's chest, but there was nothing she could do.

The dead were gone and if Sejal decided she wasn't worth the trouble, Carmine would be joining them.

Ooljee ran a paw over her face and the bobcat's skin split and shrank. She morphed back to human, the bobcat pelt limp around her neck, a fashion accessory once again.

Ooljee crouched beside Carmine, her clothes bloodied and caked in filth.

"Finally," Ooljee said, her voice breaking on the word. "What took so long?"

Sejal smiled tightly, full lips pressing into a firm line. Her eyes lit with a flash of power. The Naga reached out, in what from anyone else would have been a comforting gesture.

She ran a hand down Ooljee's face wiping away blood and dust.

"Now, now, if you'd just kept your hands to yourself, all this could have been avoided." Sejal smiled warmly. "Isn't that right, sticky fingers?"

Ooljee sniffled and wiped a hand across her eyes. "I'm sorry. Thank you, Sejal."

Carmine couldn't shake the feeling that Ooljee spoke like a child hoping to avoid punishment from a stern parent.

"At least you have good taste." Sejal patted her head like a housecat. "The mirror was a lovely gift."

The bobcat stood up, even shorter than normal, her hooker heels lost in the fight.

Palms together, hands at her forehead, she bowed at the waist three times.

Then Ooljee turned to Carmine. "Where's Rodrigo?"

Carmine raised a shaky hand and pointed at the pile of shattered glass and plywood that had been the counter.

"Over—" Her voice squeaked and she coughed. "Over there, under the rubble."

Ooljee jumped nimbly over the debris, bare feet splashing in the oily puddles. She started digging with her bare hands, tossing rubble over her shoulder.

"You look like shit," Sejal said.

Carmine looked up at the Naga. "I think I'm going to take a few months off." She'd need a week of sleep at least.

Sejal put out a hand to Carmine. "Not a problem."

Carmine stared at Sejal's hand, unwilling to take it.

The Naga winked and grinned. "I don't always bite."

Carmine took her hand and Sejal hoisted her up right like a toy doll.

When Carmine tried to pull her hand back, Sejal hung on. The Naga's eyes closed and she whispered a word.

Carmine felt heat spread from Sejal's hand and suffuse her body. When Sejal let go, Carmine realized she could stand on her own. Her knee held her weight and her face didn't feel like two pounds of raw hamburger.

"Uh, thanks," Carmine said, grinding out the words.

The snake owed her a hell of a lot more than a quick fix-it job.

Carmine doubted Sejal saw it that way, though. By

the snake's reckoning, Carmine probably owed her a favor now.

A loud sob cut off any reply Sejal was going to make.

"Shit, Rodrigo!"

Carmine went over to Ooljee. The bobcat had dug him out and she cradled his head in her lap, sobbing.

"Is he dead?" Carmine couldn't credit that he was but Ooljee was weeping so hard.

Sejal reached down and touched his cheek. "He's fine," she said.

Ooljee let out a cry of relief and hugged him harder. "O—on the roof," she sniveled. "G—go save Paco."

"What about Beto?" Carmine asked.

Ooljee shook her head.

"Goddammit!" Carmine's fists clenched and she rounded on the Naga. "What the fuck was all this for? People are dead because of you."

For a long while, Sejal regarded her silently, eyes narrowed and unreadable.

Carmine shook with rage, body taut and muscles bunched. She was dying to punch Sejal and destroy that reptilian calm.

"So much the same," Sejal said.

"What?"

Sejal took Carmine's hand. She resisted the Naga again but, even with Carmine using all her strength, Sejal pulled her arm up with all the ease of picking a penny up off the sidewalk.

She held Carmine's hand next to her own. "See, just the same."

Carmine compared her rough calloused hands with the blunt cut nails to Sejal's extravagant Swarovski encrusted manicure.

Then she saw farther, pushed no doubt by Sejal's power. Their hands turned red, dripping with blood.

Carmine could smell it, taste it, as mineral warmth she had rolled over her wolf tongue a thousand times. Savoring victory. Savoring death.

Carmine yanked her hand away but the blood didn't entirely go away. Rusty brown smears and grime remained.

"Beto Garcia and Manny Zapata's bodies will be taken home," Sejal said. "The families will each receive a generous token of thanks. Now I will go see to Paco and send him home." Sejal glided soundlessly away, the snake tail that propelled her moving over the rubble without displacing a pebble. She paused at the doorway to the repair shop. "One last thing, Carmine."

Carmine raised her head slowly. Sejal had completely derailed her fury, popping it neatly like a balloon and leaving a morose hollow ache in its place.

"What now?" She was too tired for a snide reply.

"Ishiguro's head is yours. Take it home, singe the

fur off with fire, then boil it. Eat the soup it makes. Clean the skull and keep it safe somewhere. I also recommend wearing one of his teeth."

"What?" Carmine stared at Sejal, incredulous, and swallowed an acidic lump in her throat. The thought of even touching the severed wolf head on the floor made her want to vomit. She swallowed hard and said, "I'm not doing any of that."

"She's right," Ooljee said from behind.

"Shut up."

"Then I'll come over tomorrow and help you," Sejal smiled. "It'll be fun. Girls' night in."

The Naga left, disappearing into the depths of the garage to see to Paco.

Carmine exhaled and leaned against the skeleton of a shelving unit, the contents on the floor at her feet. She focused on breathing and tried to shove aside her rising panic and gorge.

That was the sickest definition of girls' night she'd ever heard. Carmine would rather fight another dozen Okami.

"If you're going to hurl, don't do it around me," Ooljee said. Her voice was steadier now and she'd completely unearthed Rodrigo.

"What's wrong with her?" Carmine wheezed.

"Nothing, unfortunately," Ooljee said.

"But head soup?"

"You could take some of his power. The ghosting. I'd do what Sejal says if I were you."

That was the most serious Carmine had heard Ooljee sound all night and she had the prickly feeling the bobcat spoke from experience.

"I have to leave. Now." Carmine pushed herself away from the shelf and staggered toward the hole in the wall.

"I'll take Rodrigo home," Ooljee called out.

Carmine waived without turning around. She felt itchy in her skin. Too much nervous energy, too much adrenaline left over from the fight.

"And Carmine," Ooljee shouted after her, "thank you."

She didn't reply. Carmine stepped through the wall. This street looked like a war zone—or this being LA, the film set for one. The bodies were gone. Dragged away by Sejal's tigers.

But the blood remained, coagulating pools of it filling the cracks in the pavement. In the middle of the street was a shiny black limo trimmed in silver chrome.

One of the tiger sorcerers, impeccable in his tailored black suit, leaned against the door. He straightened when he saw Carmine and rushed to open the door. "Ms. Rojas, I'm to take you home."

"No thanks," Carmine said. "My car is at the Bonaventure."

"It's been driven home for you."

Carmine gritted her teeth. All these years she'd been ignorant of Sejal. Unaware of who the big boss in the skybox was. It seemed all these years, Sejal had been studying her.

But why wouldn't she? Carmine was her employee, so maybe it wasn't so strange. Or maybe it was creepy as hell.

"Then I'll walk home." Carmine darted past the limo.

"Ms. Rojas?" The tiger hesitated, eyes glancing at the garage then back to her.

She took off at a dead run. Carmine had jogged at least five miles a day and she was a block away in half a second. Around the corner in half that again.

When she was sure no one was following, sure that the tiger was well behind her, Carmine shifted on the run. She tore the T-shirt off as it split and the loaner jeans were left as a rag on the street. Her muscles bunched and lengthened as her paws and hands pounded the pavement.

The air ruffled her thick coat of fur and she gloried in the movement, inhaling the city smells as she ran—a typical but endlessly surprising symphony of car exhaust, concrete, garbage, and the heavy florals of LA's constantly blooming vegetation—all of it washing the smell of blood from her sinuses.

Home was miles away but she wanted to run. Wanted to feel her body move. Wanted the time as a wolf to let the guilt melt away.

Even if it was just for a few hours. Carmine wanted to close her eyes—to not see her hand hacking off the Okami's head.

More than anything, she didn't want to think about Sejal and the Naga's plans for her. Carmine had the awful sinking feeling the snake would show up tomorrow for a little barbeque.

The End of Round 1

ROUND 2

Chapter 1

Carmine watched the two young men circle each other on the mat.

Mick, the boy in the blue face pad and matching knuckle guards had been training in mixed martial arts a year. He'd been showing up to her karate and Krav Maga classes three or four times a week after school.

His baseline knowledge had been zero when he'd walked in the door and the only place to go was up. But he was a flyweight at best, his rangy muscles popping out on a skeletal frame, and, while Mick had improved, he wasn't a natural.

His opponent Alberto was another flyweight, bulkier than Mick but shorter by a good three inches. He came from a bad neighborhood and, unlike Mick, wasn't shy when it came to sparring.

Carmine saw Mick flinch, giving Alberto the opening. She could smell the fear on him. The acid stink of adrenaline wrinkled her sensitive nose. Alberto charged, getting Mick in a difficult wrestling hold.

"Come on, Mick, you can break the hold!" she shouted.

Across the ring Bernie, Alberto's trainer, shrugged and smiled. Alberto was aiming for the top, a career as a professional MMA fighter.

Carmine hoped the fight might teach Mick a thing or two. Maybe she was pushing too hard and would just destroy what little confidence he had.

Mick panicked and flailed in Alberto's grip. Carmine cringed, embarrassed for a split second that he was her student.

Then Mick calmed and broke the hold. He landed a few solid blows to Alberto's head, punching with fist and elbow. He retreated as Alberto swung at him.

Carmine shook her head. "Press the advantage, you had him!"

Mick glanced at her and Alberto was on him. A series of blows, head, gut, and head again, from Alberto's lightly padded fists and Mick was down.

He tapped the black gym mat and Alberto helped him up.

Bernie clapped. "Good job, Alberto."

"Thanks, coach." Alberto joined Bernie to discuss the match.

Mick came over to Carmine. His shame was obvious. Face red and shoulders hunched in defeat. He spit out his mouth guard.

"Sorry, coach," he mumbled at the ground.

"That's the worst I've seen from you in a while," Carmine said. "Know what you did wrong?"

Mick nodded.

"What's the problem?" she asked.

Mick shrugged then pulled off his headgear. His blond hair was plastered to his scalp with sweat.

Carmine wanted to grab him and shake an answer loose. "Come to my office."

She led Mick through Ronnie's Gym. The three main areas of the gym were all for fighting.

This wasn't a gym for fat soccer moms to work off the baby weight.

They exited the dojo, an open hardwood-floored space padded with gymnastic mats. They went through the main room, which was occupied by a boxing ring surrounded by punching bags.

Her closet-sized office was in the back near the entrance to the locker rooms. On the wall was a huge calendar with the dates of her classes and personal training sessions penciled in.

Carmine took the chair behind the desk and gestured to Mick to take a seat in the metal folding chair opposite. What was the Holy Trinity of teenage problems? "Is something wrong at school?"

Mick shook his head. "No."

"Girls?"

Another head shake.

Carmine moved on to her last guess. "Family?"

Mick squirmed in the chair. Finally, the right answer. How much longer would it take to drag the full story from him?

She glanced at the clock on the wall, five-thirty already. She'd been hoping to be home in time for dinner.

"So what's wrong?" Carmine gritted her teeth and added, "Maybe I can help?"

He fiddled with his knuckle guards, the rip-rip-rip of Velcro getting on her nerves.

"You don't have to tell me if you don't want to," she said, hoping he wouldn't.

She wasn't a counselor and in no position to start now. Her life was complicated enough.

"It's my mom," Mick said. "She needs an operation. A kidney transplant from my little sister and we don't have insurance. The dialysis has just about bankrupted us."

"That's terrible," Carmine said. She meant it but her voice came out flat. She hadn't given anyone condolences in so long she was out of practice. She consciously softened her voice and added, "You should be with your family. I can refund the lessons you prepaid."

Mick shook his head. "I need to train harder."

"For what?" Carmine didn't want to come out and say it but the kid would never turn pro, or even amateur. He'd be lucky to fend off incompetent muggers.

He mumbled something that to a human ear would have gone unnoticed but Carmine wasn't human. Her werewolf ears picked up the whisper of his voice.

"What was that?" she asked, not quite believing what she'd heard.

"There's these fights," he said a little louder.

The back of her neck prickled.

"You get like $5,000 for even entering."

Carmine's fist hit the metal desk like a striker on a gong. Shock almost tumbled Mick from his seat.

"What fights?" she demanded.

"Something about the jaguar shaman, a ritual battle," Mick blurted, whites showing all around his blue eyes.

She knew the fights he was talking about. She'd suspected as much from the first whisper but had hoped she was wrong.

"It's not a ritual battle," she growled, anger slightly shifting her voice to lupine. "It's a ritual slaughter. Pitting a bunch of desperate morons like you against the jaguar priests."

"But the money—"

"Is to pay for your funeral if the police find your body."

Mick's face pinched with defiance and worry. "I've been training."

"Not for this."

He shrugged. She wasn't getting through and she wasn't sure she could. Since when had a teenaged boy ever listened to reason?

"How are you going to beat a two hundred pound jaguar?"

"They turn you. If you're human you get a charm that turns you into a jaguar to even the odds."

Carmine barked out a sharp laugh, surprised anyone could be so stupid.

Mick wasn't the only one. The jaguars dangled a purse of $100,000 in front of participants just to ensure willing victims.

To Carmine's knowledge no one had ever won but that didn't mean people didn't try.

"Even as a jaguar you couldn't win. You're not good enough. You're afraid of getting hurt which is why you lose all the time."

"But being an animal changes you, doesn't it?"

Shaking her head Carmine said, "Not really. It makes you more of what you are. A coward as a human is a worse coward as a shifter."

"I'm not a coward!" Mick shot out of his seat, fists balled. The metal chair clanged against the wall of the office.

"Sit down." Carmine snarled.

Mick glanced around as if deciding whether or not to bolt and made the wise decision to sit.

"You should be scared," Carmine said. "Why are shifters banned from sports even against other shifters?"

"Yeah, I know."

"Say it."

"They kill people."

"They kill people. And do you know why we can kill people?"

"If a shifter changes, the animal takes over."

"Not exactly," Carmine said. "We still have our minds for the most part, but animals have no morals. If a shifter gets too angry or excited on the field and they change, there's no way to know if they'll kill and no way to stop them killing. And there's no guilt when they shift back.

"Those jaguar priests will kill you without a second thought and cut your heart out for their sacrifice. Is that how you want to die and leave your mom and sister alone? $5,000 won't save her or your house or anything."

He nodded slowly but kept his eyes lowered. Carmine wasn't convinced she'd gotten through. He could say anything just to get her off his back.

Unless she wanted to follow him around or lock the dumb shit in a closet, she'd have to let him leave.

"Fine. Get out." Carmine waved her hand. "If you don't show up, maybe I'll have a go at sniffing out your carcass so your mom'll have something to bury."

For a second Mick looked like he wanted to say something but the moment passed.

He stood up, moving slow as if reluctant to go, and lingered a split second at the office door before making a run for it.

Carmine exhaled. The kid wasn't her responsibility. She was only his boxing coach, not his mother.

She looked at the calendar on the wall. If the jaguars were fishing for victims, then whatever ritual they needed blood for must be soon. Where could they hold the fights this year? The victims were always found at different locations.

The cops tried to shut them down every year but they'd only managed to bust it a handful of times in the entire history of Los Angeles. But Carmine might know someone who knew someone, who would know where the slaughter was to take place.

CHAPTER 2

After their little talk, Mick cancelled his appointments with Carmine and switched over to Bernie.

He made a point of going to the gym when Carmine wasn't there and she only saw him in passing a few times over the next couple weeks.

She wanted to ask if he was going to take the jaguars up on their offer but couldn't get the words past her lips.

She did no more than grunt and nod to Mick as she passed him in the dojo or at the water fountain. A grunt and a nod was all she got in return.

Carmine kept an eye on the calendar. There was a lunar eclipse less than a week away.

A slow churning unease in her gut, along with the calendar, told her that was the date the jaguar priests had chosen.

Their rituals always coincided with something astronomical.

The day of the eclipse Carmine cleared her schedule.

Not that she had much going on. Her real job was as a prizefighter in an illegal shifter-fighting ring.

She only had two fights a month and even that was negotiable.

When she'd told Mick the dangers of shifters fighting, it hadn't been empty words.

A dozen or more opponents had perished by her teeth and claws.

Carmine called the gym from her car. She was on Highway 101, speeding south toward downtown. Maybe Mick had wised up.

"Bernie, a word."

"Sure." His voice was gruffer on the phone than in person. "What's up?"

"Have you seen Mick lately?"

"No, but I'm not surprised."

"Why? What do you know?"

"I'm harder on him than you are."

Not what she wanted to know.

Carmine's fists clenched around the steering wheel.

"The kid's been working like a dog." He paused. "Sorry, just an expression."

She ignored the phrase and the apology. "Did he say why he training so hard?"

"Nothing."

"Thanks, Bernie."

Carmine hung up.

Anxiety gripped her chest and kept squeezing. Carmine told herself Mick was old enough to make his own decisions and if he wanted to throw in the towel at seventeen, it was no never mind to her.

But the phone was still in her hand and she couldn't quite bring herself to put it down.

She flipped through the numbers on her cell and called Mick's house.

Six rings later a tired voice answered the phone.

"Hello?"

"Mrs. O'Brien?"

"Yes?"

"This is Carmine Rojas, Mick's trainer from Ronnie's Gym. Is he there?"

"No, he left early this morning."

"Did he say where he was going?"

"A movie with friends I think. He said he'd be gone all day."

"Thanks. Sorry to bother you. I thought we had an appointment."

Carmine hung up. If he was at a movie, she'd gnaw off her own tail.

Her nails drummed on the wheel. The one person who could probably tell her where the jaguar priests were holding their tourney was her boss Sejal—the snake.

Sejal owned and ran the fighting ring Carmine worked at. She'd be more than happy to point Carmine in the right direction.

For a price to be named later.

She'd only met the boss a few months ago, despite being a pit fighter at the club for three years. Carmine would have happily continued on in ignorance if Sejal hadn't needed her for a job.

Carmine would never find the jaguars on her own. Los Angeles was huge. The city bled and merged with a dozen others. Her lip curled in a silent snarl.

She took the downtown exit.

Chapter 3

There were three entrances to the fight club that Carmine knew about. All of them were located on various levels of an underground parking garage in downtown L.A.

Carmine checked the time on the dashboard as she parked on level three next to an anonymous steel door marked "Maintenance."

The "talent" entrance.

The general entrance was on level two and Sejal's private entrance was on level five. There might have been a fourth entrance.

The arena was staffed by Kitsune fox-shifters in

Sejal's employ and Carmine had never seen them enter or leave.

This early on a Saturday she couldn't be sure anyone would be there but she didn't know where Sejal lived or what body of water the Naga was paired with so her only lead was the club.

Carmine got out of the car and went to the maintenance door. The discreet lens of an electronic eye looked down at her from above the lintel.

She knocked on the door, fist pounding the metal. Echoes split the silence of the parking garage.

"Come on. I need to see Sejal."

On tiptoes she was almost face to face with the camera.

"Open up or I take the door off the hinges," she growled.

It was no idle threat. Carmine was six-three as a human and over seven feet tall as a wolf. If she changed, she could tear through the door.

The maintenance door swung open. One of the foxes let her in.

She looked at the Japanese number embroidered on his yukata. Ichi—Sejal's number one silver nine-tails.

"You aren't expected," he said.

"Take me to Sejal," she told him.

The fox let out a long, weary sigh. "If it keeps you from battering down the door, fine."

She followed him through the plain corridors of the fight club's backstage.

Hallways she knew by heart. Carmine had the urge to shove the fox aside so she could pick up the pace.

But what the Kitsune lacked in muscle they made up for in magic and Ichi could easily stop her from seeing Sejal without laying a hand on her.

They crossed the lobby and Ichi opened a door that read "Janitor" but really led to Sejal's private box.

Ichi nodded to the two hefty tiger sorcerers guarding the door to Sejal's waiting room.

The sorcerers looked human but in an instant they could shift into massive tigers.

They were Sejal's loyal army and Carmine still had no idea how many she commanded. There seemed to be a new pair every time she came.

The waiting room was an extravagant, dimly lit, Moroccan tableau mixed with a heavy dose of drapery. A jewel-toned riot of magenta, blue, and peacock sari silk covered plain concrete walls.

Turkish rugs warmed the floor and a scattering of throw pillows the size of small couches completed the furnishing.

Carmine coughed.

As if on cue, the overwhelming stink of sandalwood incense clung to everything. Little cones of it burned in glass lamps strung from the ceiling.

Under the choking sandalwood was the heavy swamp tang of reptile.

"Wait here," Ichi said.

He pointed to the pillows and disappeared into Sejal's inner sanctum.

Another plain steel door framed by two more steroidal tigers.

She wanted to pace but didn't think walking back and forth in front of a couple big cats was a good idea. Carmine had seen them in action once and that was enough.

A few minutes later Ichi came back and held the door for Carmine.

"Ms. Johar will see you."

Carmine darted through the door. Eager to leave the scrutiny of the tigers.

The door shut behind her and Carmine was alone in a hot room with some thirty-five feet of Naga.

Sejal slithered into the light of the red heat lamp bulbs she favored.

As if L.A. wasn't hot enough, the Naga kept her skybox at a sweltering ninety degrees.

Sejal grinned. "What a lovely surprise."

The snake-shifter was her usual flamboyant self. A hot pink bikini top and sari covered her top half.

The rest of her, from the waist down, was polished, glinting scales in myriad shades of brown.

Carmine nodded stiffly. She was never sure of Sejal's intentions.

The Naga always seemed to be in good humor but power poured off her in sheets.

Exactly what she was capable of Carmine wasn't sure.

She'd only had hints of the Naga's power in the past but no other shifter's power raised her hackles like Sejal's. Her mere presence tingled like static electricity.

"I need information," Carmine said.

Sejal gazed heavenward in exaggerated exasperation. "Information? I was hoping for a social call."

The Naga slithered toward Carmine, her smile predatory.

"The jaguar priests hold their sacrifice today," Carmine said quickly.

Sejal froze for a second then defrosted. It was enough to tell Carmine she knew about the fights. Maybe even the location.

"You don't get enough to kill here?"

"No. I just need to know where."

As Sejal moved, so did her tail. Carmine could see the coils moving closer, boxing her in.

"Why?" Sejal tapped a hot pink crystal encrusted fingernail against the diamond stud in her nose. "And tell the truth."

A growl vibrated in Carmine's chest. "A kid I

coach is entering. I think. He's seventeen and stupid and desperate and he's going to die."

"And maybe being seventeen and stupid isn't a good enough reason?"

Sejal stopped moving inches from Carmine. Her forked tongue tasted the air, the points flickering so close Carmine could feel the movement on her skin like butterfly kisses. She flinched and turned her head. "No, it's not a good reason to die."

The Naga pressed closer. Her full lips pulled into a wide smile that showed off slender fangs.

Carmine knew better than to try and bolt. When she wanted, Sejal could move like lightning, faster than the eye could see.

The sharp point of her manicured nail poked Carmine's breastbone.

Sejal let out a throaty laugh. "Did your heart grow three sizes today?"

"No," Carmine shot back.

"You care," Sejal sing-songed, "You're a niiice person."

"Shut up!" Carmine batted her hand away. "Can you tell me where they are, or not?"

Sejal laughed again and backed off a fraction of an inch. "As my champion, you should learn patience."

This wasn't the only time Sejal had mentioned this "champion" bullshit.

Carmine found it as disconcerting as the first. "I'm not your champion."

"Yes, you are." Sejal held up a hand cutting off further comment. "We can argue all day or we can go find your student."

"We?"

"I have a charm that will guide me to the fight. I can use it and come with you or I can impart it to you."

The last time Sejal imparted a charm to Carmine it had meant a full kiss on the mouth.

With tongue.

"Let's go," she said.

Then Sejal changed. Right in front of Carmine. The Naga didn't even look embarrassed. The yards and yards of snake tail retreated magically into her body. As it disappeared, the scales grew hazy and faded to nothing.

Less than five seconds later she stood on long bronze legs. Her sari formed a pink mini-skirt. "Come on."

Sejal waved Carmine over to the private entrance to the owner's box.

The door to the parking garage was hidden behind more gauzy curtains.

A flight of stairs led to the parking garage where a black limo waited, idling by the door. Sejal hadn't called for the car, at least not by visible means.

Telepathy maybe.

Carmine had no idea how Sejal commanded her troops.

A tiger sorcerer climbed out of the driver's side. The limo rocked on its suspension when his bulk was removed.

He came around and held open the passenger side door for them.

Sejal got into the limo first and Carmine averted her eyes.

Panties didn't come with the shape shift and Sejal seemed to have no problem going commando.

She scooted to the far end of the leather seat and patted the spot next to her.

"Sit, sit," Sejal said.

Carmine got in and the tiger shut the door. "So where is this thing?" she asked.

Anxiety curled through her gut. Mick could already be dead.

"Give me a second," Sejal told her.

The tiger got behind the wheel and put the car in drive. Sejal stuck out her tongue and touched the sharp pink tip of her fingernail to it. Blue-gray smoke drifted from the indentation.

A spicy scent tickled Carmine's nose, like vinegar and *habeñero* peppers. She sneezed in rapid-fire succession three times as the smoke dissipated.

With the touch of a button Sejal rolled down the limo's tinted back window. Her tongue flickered.

"Go left when you hit the street," she told the driver.

The limo pulled out of the parking garage and they were on their way, Sejal's tongue tasting the air at every stoplight.

Forty minutes of freeway on the 110 went by and Carmine grew more restless.

They passed the exits for Inglewood, Gardena, and Carson. Any farther and they'd drive into the Pacific Ocean.

Finally Sejal tasted the air again. "Exit here."

At last.

Carmine looked out the window. There was a sign for the Port of Los Angeles.

The port may have been a mile off but already the smell of diesel and burning oil blew in the open window.

Carmine growled. The port was perfect for the sacrifices.

The soup of pollution hovering over it would confound any shifter's nose and the ocean was the perfect dumpsite for a load of bodies.

Sejal poked her head out the window. Black hair lashed against her face coming undone from her up-do. Her forked tongue tasted the toxic breeze.

"Take the next left," she told the driver.

He nodded.

Residential neighborhoods gave way to warehouses. Big rig trucks blasted past with increasing frequency, fumes pouring into the limo.

The smell made Carmine's temples throb. She wished Sejal could roll up the window. No shifter Carmine knew lived anywhere near the port or its adjacent cities.

Sejal gave her driver a few more directions and the road dead-ended at a fenced in parking lot. A warehouse rose above the cars and steel shipping containers stacked near the building.

The gate was padlocked but no guards were to be seen.

The limo pulled over to the side of the road and parked. Sejal opened her door before the driver could get out and Carmine followed her lead.

Hot, late afternoon sun pounded the bare expanse of tarmac. Only a few dozen cars were parked in the shadow of the building. A cool ocean breeze, tasting of tanker oil, stirred the air.

Sejal pointed. "This is it."

She looked around. Sejal's bare feet slapped on the pavement as she approached. She held up a hand and muttered something. The gates blew open, chain and padlock both severed neatly in half.

Even if her nose didn't work, Carmine kept her ears pricked. In the distance, she heard heavy machinery and boat horns. Overhead seagulls cried, looking for garbage to eat.

"They must be inside," Sejal said. Her tongue waved. "This place tastes like blood and burning."

Carmine bolted for the warehouse. Sejal called out behind her but Carmine didn't listen.

She followed the wall of the cinderblock exterior until she found a door. She put her ear to it. Nothing.

The doorknob refused to turn. Locked. Carmine growled and let herself change, just a little. Just enough to bulk up.

She threw herself at the steel and felt it buckle. Again, and the hinges squealed. It gave on the fourth attack, hinges ripping from the frame.

Carmine took a deep breath to reel in the change before she went full wolf.

As soon as Carmine stepped over the threshold, she felt the tingle of a ward across her skin.

She heard music, piping and harsh with a low drumbeat keeping time.

The thick iron scent of blood and cooking meat flooded her nose, drowning out the fumes of the port. The smell wet her mouth. She felt a rush of hunting instincts and sharp hunger.

Carmine followed her nose through darkened

glassed in offices until the hallways ended in an open warehouse.

The roof soared three stories above the massive hollow interior. Pollution-tinted orange sunlight slanted in through milky windows.

In the center was a chain link cage. Thirty-by-thirty. Enough room to let the jaguar's prey run around a little and get the blood going.

A crowd of worshippers surrounded the cage, their eyes fixed on the spectacle within.

Carmine glanced right and saw the source of the heady barbeque aroma.

Three jaguar priests in human form clustered around a stone alter shaped like a man lying on his back.

Fire smoked in an iron brazier. Roasting on the coals were human hearts, carved from the chests of the victims stacked beside the altar like cordwood.

The screeching yowl of a cat rose above the musicians and chants of the priests.

Carmine turned back in time to see a skinny, pale-yellow jaguar rebound off the chain link.

She snarled and ran, shoving through the crowd, throwing aside bystanders. They smelled human and were no real threat to her. Angry shouts went up in her wake but Carmine didn't care. Rage took hold of her, pushing her close to changing.

She reached the cage as a huge prowling jaguar roared at his smaller prey.

Carmine sniffed.

As she thought.

The starving yellow jaguar cowering against the chain link was Mick.

The back of Carmine's neck tingled. She spun around. A short man ran at her wielding a stubby piece of rebar.

Carmine charged before he could swing and punched him in the face. She felt the bridge of his hatchet nose shatter under her knuckles. He hit the floor, out cold.

"Get the wolf!" the high priest shouted from the altar.

The other priests touched the jaguar tooth necklaces strung around their throats.

Swirling gray-green smoke curled around the priests and less than a second later two big cats were stalking through the crowd.

The human supplicants wisely scattered and ran, heading for an exit or higher ground.

The high priest stuck two fingers in his mouth and whistled. Summoning reinforcements. Carmine wondered briefly how many more there were. It didn't matter.

She grinned and changed. Her body grew and

twisted, joints shifted, and muscles doubled in size. Her T-shirt split down the back and her jeans ripped at the seams. Sleek black fur covered naked skin in a shiny pelt.

The first jaguar leapt and she swiped a clawed hand through the air. The blow connected, bone deep gashes poured blood. The cat hit the ground writhing in pain. A second jaguar slammed into her.

She fell to all fours as the jaguar clawed her back, trying to get a grip on her neck with its teeth. Carmine rolled and drove the back of her skull into the cat's face as her elbow jabbed its ribs.

Screeching, the cat twisted beneath her, struggling to get away. Carmine leapt up, spun, and brought her hind leg down on its skull with shattering force.

One down and—she looked around—four cats circled, including the one with ground meat for a face.

Three leapt at once.

The jaguar with the meat grinder face hung back. Ten years of martial arts training took hold without a thought.

She caught one jaguar mid leap and threw it into a second cat. The third rammed her stomach but she was ready for it. Carmine went with the blow and kicked from beneath, hooked claws tearing open the cat's underbelly. A final kick and it went flying, a comet tail of blood streaking behind it.

The other two cats recovered, shaking their heads as they untangled their limbs. Both cats roared, flashing ivory fangs.

Carmine's ears twitched. The whisper of soft paws stalked behind her. Meat Grinder. She didn't turn.

The two jaguars in front of her split. One struck left, the other right. She kept both cats in sight and waited. They tensed.

The weight of Meat Grinder hit her back, two hundred pounds of lithe muscle with a running start.

A long burn of pain streaked across her back and sides as the cat anchored its claws in her flesh.

Carmine gripped the cat's leg and flipped it overhead. Its claws tore out of her and she yelped in pain.

The cat hit the concrete floor hard and Carmine dropped on top of it.

Her elbow smashed the jaguar's ribs driving the bone shards onto its lungs. Crimson foam bubbled from its nose and mouth.

Yowling like a siren, one of the last two jaguars leapt while she was down.

Maybe it thought coming in high gave it an advantage. Maybe it thought she wasn't ready. Mostly it was just pissed off and unused to a real opponent.

Carmine caught the cat as it landed. Her paw-hands circled the cat's wrists and she held it firm.

Her jaws parted, showing long canines of her own.

The cats weren't the only one with impressive ivories. Carmine snapped her jaws shut, closing on the jaguar's throat.

The cat struggled hard, hind legs raking across her stomach and thighs.

Too far away to disembowel her, but close enough to hurt like a bitch. Blood poured into her mouth as her teeth found the carotid artery.

Her head shook, tearing the wound wider and deeper. Her tongue lapped up the mineral rich gush. Iron, salt, and a hint of copper.

The jaguar convulsed.

She tossed aside the carcass and stood up, ready for the last cat.

A voice rang out echoing through the warehouse.

"Coatl!"

"Coatl!"

She looked around. The last jaguar hung back, skulking toward the high priest still at his altar.

Everyone froze.

The voice had come from above. Carmine followed the sound to a group of worshippers still lingering on the elevated catwalks a story above.

The jaguar in the cage with Mick hissed at something behind Carmine. She turned.

Sejal was snaking her way toward them. Carmine's eyes narrowed and her lip curled over her canines.

How convenient of Sejal to show up now after all the heavy lifting was done.

The high priest rushed over to meet Sejal.

"What are you doing here Coatl?" His copper skin was slicked with sweat and Carmine could smell his acid rage ten feet away. "Is this animal yours?"

Carmine snarled at the priest but Sejal put herself between them.

The Naga reached up and put a hand on her shoulder.

"She is indeed my champion."

Carmine's snarl cut off and she gave Sejal a sidelong glance.

"The bitch has killed four of my *chac*." He gestured the cooling remains of the jaguars.

"I'm sorry, Ah Khin—"

He spit on the dusty floor. "Sorry?"

"—But she only came to claim her student," Sejal finished.

"Who is it?"

"That jaguar there, the one cowering in his own piss. He's just a boy. A minor," Sejal said, her voice cold as her blood.

The Ah Khin stiffened. He paled, ash touching the red of his skin. Carmine's gaze went from Sejal to the priest and back again. How far did Sejal's territory extend that she held sway all the way to the coast?

A hundred questions swam through Carmine's mind. One day she'd have to start asking.

"We had an agreement, Ah Khin."

Sejal's voice was a husky threatening whisper that carried clearly through the hot air.

"He lied to us." The Ah Khin said.

Sejal's tongue flickered as if tasting his words. She smiled wide, showing slender fangs, and a chill zipped down Carmine's spine.

"No he didn't," Sejal said. "We'll take the boy and you will not seek reprisal. You will obey our agreement. Now, unlock the cage door and tell your *chac* to stand down."

The Ah Khin grunted sullenly. He walked past Sejal and Carmine, giving them a wide berth, and pulled a key from the white belt around his waist.

He unlocked the door and the last jaguar slunk out of the cage, taking his place at the high priest's side.

Mick didn't move. His pale cat body was pressed into the chain link, golden eyes wide, the pupil's tiny pinpricks.

Sejal gestured to Carmine.

She snorted and ducked into the cage. Mick hissed at her but Carmine ignored him. She could smell the fear on him.

She grabbed him by the scruff of the neck and pulled him out.

Sejal inclined her head, "We'll be going now. Next time stick to the covenants."

Mick hung from Carmine's fist, limp as a dishrag. His breathing was ragged and hoarse.

She dragged him over the concrete, not caring if he got banged up. He should be grateful she bothered to show up.

Sejal slithered away from the carnage without a backward glanced but Carmine turned around, as she smelled the sharp spice of their change.

The two jaguar priests watched them leave. The Ah Khin glowered at Carmine and Sejal.

She could almost feel the heat of his hatred on her back.

The head priest gestured at his eyes then at Carmine in the universal sign for "I'm watching you."

She snapped her teeth and licked her chops. Let them come if they dared.

Carmine followed Sejal back through the warehouse along the route she'd entered.

They stepped out into the parking lot and Sejal led her to the limo.

The driver had pulled up as close to the building as he could.

"Change back. I don't want you scratching up the leather."

Carmine whined and gestured at herself.

"Oh yeah, you're naked under all that fur," Sejal grinned.

She snapped her fingers and the driver got out of the limo.

He went to the trunk and pulled out what looked like a bolt of shimmering emerald green fabric.

Mick stirred at last and Carmine dropped him to the pavement. His nose twitched and his eyes focused as he pushed himself up on all fours. Ears flattened in terror, he looked up at his rescuers.

"Take off that ridiculous necklace," Sejal ripped the necklace off, heedless of his fangs. The collar snapped and Sejal tossed it to the ground.

In a puff of smoke Mick was himself again. He crouched on the asphalt wearing only a white loincloth and a jaguar skin shrug. He gaped at them, still fearful, eyes round.

Carmine made a gentle growl. Mick's eyes fixed on her, traveled up and down the seven feet of black wolf, and then rolled back in his head. He fainted dead.

Sejal laughed but Carmine just grunted.

"Somebody's had a little too much excitement for one day," Sejal cooed with mock parental concern. "Does little man need a nap? Put him in the limo."

Carmine shook her head. She took the sari from the driver and headed behind a cargo container.

A few seconds later and she was human again.

Carmine wrapped the embroidered silk around herself as best she could but instead of the intricate folds, she just wound it around herself like a towel. The silk clung to the bloody scratches covering her body and she hoped Sejal didn't want the sari back in mint condition.

Sejal giggled as Carmine came back. "I'll show you how to wear a sari sometime. Come on."

"Mick in the car?"

"Sleeping like a baby."

Sejal climbed into the limo with the requisite vag-flash.

Carmine pulled the silk around herself as she got in even though there was no one there to see.

"So where does he live?" Sejal poked the unconscious Mick with her big toe.

Carmine gave her an address in Culver City. The driver overheard and pulled away from the warehouse.

She watched it dwindle in the distance and rubbed her forehead.

She could still taste the blood in her mouth and her stomach rumbled. She hadn't eaten since lunch and the sun was lowering in the sky.

"We'll go back to the club after we deposit boy wonder."

"He's a good kid. A shit fighter, but a good person." Carmine said. "He needed the money to get his mom a kidney transplant."

"He's lucky to go home in one piece," Sejal observed.

CHAPTER 4

Carmine gazed at the calendar hanging on the office wall. She found a 5 p.m. opening and penciled in the name Amerie, a new student interested in mixed martial arts training.

There was a knock at the open door. Carmine glanced over.

Mick.

She should have smelled him but hadn't been paying attention.

He smiled at the wall behind her, too shy to meet her eyes.

"Hey, coach."

She lifted her chin to get a whiff of him. He smelled like hospital antiseptic tinged with fear.

"Ola, Mick," she said. "What can I do for you?"

He ran his fingers through his shaggy blond hair. "I—I wanted to thank you for everything. You and that other lady. You were right. I was stupid to fight the jaguars."

"That's the definition of seventeen."

Mick finally looked at her. A shadow crossed his face. Fear.

He'd seen her as a wolf and now that's all he'd ever see. A gore soaked werewolf tearing the throat out of a big cat.

"I—I just thought I should tell you in person."

Carmine nodded. "I'm glad you're okay."

Mick hovered in the doorway. Carmine waited for him to say more.

"My mom got her kidney," he said, his voice choked. "She's going to be fine. I can't thank you enough for the money."

Carmine's eyebrows convulsed. She pressed her face back to normal, grateful Mick was staring at the floor.

Her surprise cooled to wintry knowing. Sejal. Maybe she'd paid for the operation herself.

Maybe she'd take the money out of Carmine's winnings.

Or worse yet, maybe she'd forced the jaguar priests to pay up.

The last thought sent a river of ice through Carmine's veins.

"I'm glad." Lucky her, the words came out steadier than she thought she could manage.

"I'm—um." His mouth turned down and he looked at her. "I'm sorry. I'm going to quit training. Mom needs my help and I got a part time job and I never was any good at martial arts anyway."

Carmine waved away his excuses. "It's okay. You don't owe me anything."

Without warning, Mick lunged. Carmine stiffened as he hugged her with all his wiry strength.

"I owe you my life, coach."

She was too stunned to return the hug and stood awkwardly with her arms out as he let go.

"Thanks again. Thank you."

He flashed a wide sincere grin that warmed his narrow features.

"Good luck." Carmine said.

"Thanks," he repeated and left the office.

Carmine felt her own rusty and unused smile muscles stretch. She let herself feel good for almost a full minute before turning back to the calendar.

The weekends were printed in red ink. How appropriate. Today was Saturday and she was on tonight. Star of the fight club. Her smile turned grim if no less genu-ine.

    She might be able to beg an audience with Sejal.

    Time to start asking questions.

                The End of Round 2

About the Author

Che Gilson is the author of several graphic novels including *Avigon: Gods and Demons* from Image Comics, and *Dark Moon Diary* from Tokyopop. Her short stories have been published online in *Luna Station Quarterly* issue 14 and *Drops of Crimson* (which is no longer operating).

She draws copious amounts of Pokémon fan art and is working on multiple novels including a contemporary fantasy about tea and witches and two children's books.